Missing ~~Wife~~ Life

Nikki Perry & Kirsty Roby

1st edition, 2021

Edited by Evan Chan

ISBN 978-0-473-60319-9 (paperback)

ISBN 978-0-473-60321-2 (Kindle)

ISBN 978-0-473-60320-5 (Epub)

Cover design and layout by Yummy Book Covers

Typeset in Droid Serif, 10.5pt

Sometimes all you need is a good friend
and a full tank of gas.

Acknowledgements

Firstly, thank you - the reader. We hope you enjoy this book as much as we enjoyed writing it.

Thanks to Eva Chan for her quick and efficient editing and to Enni of Yummy Book Covers for another wonderful cover.

Much gratitude to our family, especially the kids, who had to put up with our endless hours of phone calls about plots and characters while we ignored them.

As an aside, we have to point out that to our knowledge, Captain Cook's hand was never preserved and neither does the town of Bode exist.

The Missing ~~Wife~~ Life

Chapter one

Dominion Post:

FLAT PARTY OUT OF CONTROL; SIX ARRESTS MADE

Police were called to a Kilbirnie address when a student party raged out of control last night. Angry neighbours reported bottles being thrown, street fights and loud music. One woman, who wanted to remain anonymous, said that it was usually a quiet neighbourhood but the beginning of the academic year saw a rise in obnoxious behaviour. All six people taken into custody were released this morning and no further charges have been laid.

When Anna woke, her face was squashed against a couch cushion that felt like it hadn't been washed since the seventies. There was a small pool of drool under her cheek. She could smell an unpleasant mix of slow-drying dog, ramen noodles and feet. Her stomach churned and her head pulsed inside her skull. Somewhere someone moaned and then a door banged loudly against a wall.

"Are you the mum?" a voice above her asked. She turned her head slightly, cracked open an eye. A skinny young guy with ripped jeans and a man bun hovered over her.

"Baz asked me to give you the keys," he said. "The van's out front."

He put a set of keys down beside her, the keyring a faded red casino chip. She closed her eyes and when she opened them again, he was gone. Her brain swirled slowly, bile creeping up the back of her parched throat. A matted strand of hair was stuck like hardened porridge against the side of her face. She shut her eyes.

"Far out, where are we?" someone croaked. There was a rustling sound beside her, then clattering glass and a bottle rolled across the floor, spilling out brown sludge and a bent cigarette butt onto the worn rug.

"Whose flat is this? And where are my shoes?" The voice wasn't familiar. Outside, someone started up a car with a very bad muffler. Anna forced herself to sit up. Acid burned up her throat.

A woman sat across from her on an old mustard-coloured La-Z-Boy. Her dark hair was sticking up on one side of her head like a bad attempt at a Princess Leia bun. She wore a pair of mum jeans and a slightly crumpled floral print shirt with an oversized pink knit cardigan. She looked familiar, but Anna struggled to remember who she was.

"I feel a bit sick," the woman announced, standing up shakily and moving towards the kitchen where she paused to look at the stack of dishes piled haphazardly in the sink.

Anna took a minute to look around. She had come down to Wellington to help Ben shift into his flat. This was not it. Her son's flat was no palace, but this was more like a squat. Mould grew up the corner of one wall where a shelf made of bricks and old pallets housed a dead cactus and several old takeaway boxes. A road cone sat beside the hallway door, a pair of black boxers draped across the top. On the coffee table and across the floor were empty cans and liquor bottles. There was a suspicious dark patch of something on the rug that Anna avoided identifying. She tried not to breathe in.

The woman returned, sipping from a filmy-looking jar filled with water.

"This is embarrassing, but I can't remember your name," she said. "Sorry."

"Anna," Anna said. Her voice was raspy.

"I'm Faith, Rachel's mum."

Ah, this made sense. Rachel was one of Ben's new flatmates. She had a vague recollection of meeting Faith the day before when she helped them with Ben's mattress.

"How on the earth did we end up here?" Faith asked. "All I remember is going with Keiley to get more tonic and snacks."

Anna tried to picture Keiley. Was she the other flatmate? She thought perhaps she was the one with the lip piercing and the streaks of green in her hair, but there seemed to be a lot of uni girls with K names.

They had helped the kids move in. She remembered that now. Remembered ordering pizzas and a few of the kids' friends had turned up with some drinks. She and Faith had been reluctantly invited to join them. They played 'Never have I ever'. That was where things got hazy.

Anna rubbed her hand across her face, peeling the concreted hair away and then looked around for her phone. She looked again at the keys next to her on the stained couch.

"Do you have a van?" she asked Faith.

"Oh no, the *van*," Faith said, putting her hand across her mouth. "Surely that wasn't for real?" She had a horrified sort of look on her face. Anna's stomach was clenching with a weird sense of dread. Something was prickling at the back of her mind.

Faith took off for the front door, flinging it open onto the street. Fresh air and sunlight welcomed them. Anna stood to follow her. There was a pair of ballet flats half hidden under the sofa, Faith's missing shoes, she assumed. She was still wearing her heels.

"*No!*" Faith said loudly. Then, "No," very quietly.

Out on the street, parked at a weird angle across the driveway, sat a badly painted bubblegum-pink Hiace van. 'Rick's Plumbing' was written on the side. Underneath it; 'All cisterns go since 1998'.

"Don't you remember? Last night," Faith said. "We bought a van. Together."

◇

They wandered warily down the steps and approached the van. Anna tested the key and found it fitted the creaky passenger door. It would seem they were indeed in possession of a pink, Scooby-Doo-style vehicle, only with more rust.

She slid open the side door. Inside, it smelt vaguely of mouse and burnt rope. The back had been shoddily renovated and there were two skinny beds down the length, fitted sheets and duvets with Disney characters on them covering the mattresses. A small set of drawers was wedged at the top between them. Navy curtains were attached to the grimy windows and under one bed was a plastic storage box containing kitchen necessities, a rather threadbare towel, a few cans of baked beans and a roll of toilet paper. A box of corroded tools and a bag of rusted washers wedged into a side panel were perhaps left over from the van's plumbing heyday.

Anna closed the door and turned to Faith.

"I'm sorry, I just can't process this right now. I need coffee and a Berocca and a minute to think."

Faith laughed, sounding nervous. "I agree. Well, a tea anyway. Shall we find a cafe and get our bearings?"

They looked around the street, as if a cafe might magically appear a few houses down.

"Shit. I don't even know what suburb we're in," Anna confessed.

"I need to find my purse and have a wee," Faith said. "Shall we go back inside and see if anyone can tell us where we are?"

They headed back into the flat. The smell seemed worse after the fresh air. Anna went down the hall, opening doors to find someone awake or a bathroom.

The bathroom had starry lino and a peach sink clogged with regurgitated pizza. The toilet door was blocked by a ripe body, snoring loudly. Something scuttled away against the skirting boards as she opened doors.

When she returned, Faith was pulling her phone out from under the couch.

"Trust me when I say you want to wait to use a loo," she told her. "And according to the trio I found in the end bedroom, there's a cafe two streets over that does good cheese scones."

"Sounds like a plan. I could murder a cheese scone and I can hold on for the bathroom if it's that bad. Shoot, my phone's dead," Faith said with a frown.

"You can use mine if you want," Anna told her.

"Thanks, after I've had a wee will be fine. I kind of want to get out of here."

◇

They found the cafe easily enough, a short walk from the flat, and nabbed a table outside, happy for the fresh air, despite the cold. Anna sat and fished her phone out of her bag while Faith used the ladies. There were eight missed calls, most from her husband Greg, and a lot of texts all from Ben wondering where she was. She rang him first.

"Mum. Where are you? Dad's been ringing me all morning."

"Sorry, hun, I'll ring him soon. I'm in a cafe with Rachel's mum."

"Where did you guys go? Oh man, you guys were a crack-up last night. You never came back with the tonic though? Are you all sweet?"

"Ahh, yes, we ahh ..." Anna's phone buzzed with another call. Greg. "That's your dad ringing, I'd better talk to him."

"Yeah, okay, talk to you later." Ben hung up and Anna accepted the waiting call.

"Where the *fuck* are you?" Greg yelled down the phone just as Faith returned to the table. "I was waiting at the god-damn airport for almost an hour and you weren't even on the bloody flight. What the hell, Anna?"

"Sorry," Anna mouthed to Faith, as she sat down with a carafe of water and two glasses. She knew Faith could hear him and her face was burning with embarrassment. She looked at her watch. It was already after eleven. Her flight back to Auckland had been at nine.

"I'm so sorry, I missed my flight," she said.

"No shit, Sherlock," Greg bellowed. "What the hell is going on? We were supposed to be at the appointment at eleven."

Bugger. The marriage counsellor. Anna tried to think what to tell him. How was she going to explain that she'd had far too much to drink at a uni flat party and somehow ended up in some scody dive of a flat, now the owner of a shit-heap van. Before she could get a word out though, Greg was yelling again.

"I don't have the bloody time for this shit. Some of us have work to do. Just get on another flight and get your own bloody way back from the airport." Then he hung up. Arsehole, Anna thought. Even if it was technically her fault.

She held out the phone to Faith as the waitress arrived with their scones and hot drinks.

"Did you want to make some calls?

"Actually, I think maybe I need to get my head on straight before I ring Daniel," Faith said, tipping a sachet of sugar into her cup.

"Yeah, that's a good point. I have to confess, I have no memory of us buying the van. Or much else to be honest." Anna grimaced.

"Yeah, the van. It seemed like such a good idea at the time. Mind you, he never said it was so ... pink." She sipped her coffee. "So, as I recall, we were talking about how I'm going to see my brother in the South Island, and you were saying you wanted to go down to see your ... boys ... in Christchurch?"

"Boy and girl," Anna said. "Twins. Cameron and Niamh."

"Right, and we'd been saying how the reason we were so drunk after playing 'Never have I ever' was because we hadn't lived enough, and that led to how we should do a road trip together." That did sound a bit familiar actually, Anna thought. "Then that nice guy with the mullet said he was selling his van, and we could have it for eight hundred and I hadn't booked any flights yet, and so, yeah, we did it." Faith drained the rest of her coffee and poured more water into their glasses.

"Good grief. Okay, so what do we do with it now?" Anna asked, scrummaging in her bag and finding a sheet of Panadol. "Want some?"

"Yes, please." They downed the painkillers and then sat in silence.

"My issue is, I really do need to get to Invercargill," Faith said, "and that van money was all I had to use for the flights."

"Do you think this guy will buy it back?" Anna asked doubtfully. "Do we even know his name?"

"I think maybe Barry? Or Barney? Benny? It started with a B."

"Shit."

They both looked at each other and then laughed.

"We're worse than the kids," Faith said.

"I think we need more caffeine."

◇

Eventually they decided to walk back to the flat and see if anyone knew Barry/Benny/Barney.

No one was home, the door locked.

"Where are you staying?" Anna asked.

"Oh gosh, I'm at the Travelodge and I'm supposed to be

checked out by now."

"Yeah, me too. I'm at the James Cook. I think we should go grab our bags and then we can go back to the kids' flat and work out what to do."

"Okay. Maybe someone there will want a van?" They looked over at said van. It now had what looked like a parking ticket but was hopefully a flyer on its front windscreen. It seemed very pink and patchy in the midday sun.

"Who's driving?" Anna asked.

"Well, if you don't mind?" Faith said. "I'm not a very confident driver, and I hate driving in cities."

They climbed in and looked around. Apart from a Post Malone air freshener hanging from the rearview mirror it was pretty sparse. Anna put the key in the ignition and turned it, half expecting it not to turn over. But it roared to life, along with the stereo, which was belting out some Australian rap artist singing about good pussy. Anna quickly pushed the power button, cutting him off mid-sentence.

"Right, here we go." It had been a while since she'd driven a manual and they lurched down the road, bunny-hopping a few times before they swung out into the Wellington traffic.

Chapter two

Ben was sitting out in the small overgrown front courtyard wrapped in a blanket when they returned to the flat. He ran a hand across his jaw and then through his floppy blond hair to pull it away from his face. He looked like he was sporting a hangover but got up and hugged Anna and then, after hesitating for a moment, gave Faith a hug too. Rachel had gone to uni and the other flatmates were both still asleep.

"I heard you arrive. Before I even saw you," Ben said looking pointedly at the bright-pink van. "What the fuck is that monstrosity?"

"Yes, the van. It would seem Faith and I bought it last night," Anna sighed. "By the way, do you know a guy called Benny or Barney or something? He was at the flat we ended up at in Kilbirnie. I don't think he lived there though."

"Nope, don't think so. That's not much to go on, Mum. How did you end up in Kilbirnie anyway? I thought you were coming back here, then I thought you must have bailed and gone back to the hotel."

"We really should have," Faith said as she plopped herself onto one of the cheap plastic patio chairs. She rubbed absently at her temple looking tired. "I doubt Barney or Boris or whoever we bought it from is going to give us our money back, even if we could find him. It's probably already spent. Do you know anyone who wants to buy a pink ex-plumbing-now-shoddy camper van?"

Ben scratched his chin. "Yeah, nah, probably not. You could try and sell it on Vic Deals, I guess."

"That might be our best option, but how long will it take to sell? I'm meant to be heading to Invercargill. I'd drive down but I can't afford to pay you out for your half, Anna."

Anna's mind whirled. As fast as it could given her current hungover state. The thought of going home and dealing with Greg wasn't exactly appealing. She'd obviously been talking about going to visit the twins to Faith the night before. She hadn't seen Cameron since he'd gone back to Christchurch after Christmas and Niamh had stayed down there to work so it had been months since she'd seen her.

She didn't need the money, she could just let Faith take the van, but she'd said she wasn't a confident driver. And then there was the shambles of her marriage waiting at home for her. She had a sudden longing to see the kids, and maybe to talk to them about what was going on with their father, just to sound them out so it wasn't a complete shock for them.

"What were you thinking of doing?" Anna asked Faith. "Are you going to drive straight to Invercargill?"

"I haven't really thought about it, but I can take a few days to get there. As long as I'm there by Saturday week. There won't be much to do on my own so I suppose I'll just drive and stop where it's convenient. I'd ask Rachel to come with me but she can't really take time off from uni. If I just take it easy and stop heaps I'll be okay. It's probably not that much different than driving a car."

Anna didn't think Faith looked that convinced.

"I might have to make one of those playlists on my phone to keep me company," Faith added.

"I don't suppose you'd want some human company?" Anna asked her. "I mean, I know we don't really know each other but I promise you I'm a reasonably decent person. That is, if you wouldn't mind me tagging along? And I don't mind driving."

"Really?" Faith looked relieved. "I'm happy for you to come with me if you want to. It could even be fun."

"Then stuff it, I'm going to go with you."

"Really? You're actually going to do it?" Faith asked.

"Sure, as long as you're okay going via Christchurch. I can't remember exactly what we talked about doing last night but I haven't seen much of the South Island so why not, right?"

"Have you asked Dad about this?"

"I don't have to *ask* your father anything, Ben," Anna told him. "I'm my own person." The children didn't really know the extent of their marital problems. In fact, Anna had told Greg she wanted a divorce and he, reluctant to sell the house and give her half what the business was worth she suspected, had been digging his toes in. Now that Ben had left home for uni, Anna was determined to make him see their marriage was well and truly over. Done and dusted. A dead duck.

"Okay, I need to make a call. Do you mind if I plug my phone in to charge it?" Faith said getting up and heading inside, grabbing her phone and charger from her handbag.

"Look, Ben," Anna sighed after she'd left. "Things haven't been great between your dad and me for a while. I'm going to go down and see the twins and then I think I'll take a bit of time out travelling with Faith before I go back and sort things out with him."

Ben shrugged. "Yeah, fair enough. I mean it's pretty obvious you haven't been getting along. Kind of thought that when you moved into the spare room, to be honest." He ran his hand through his hair. "Whatever though, it's your business."

"I guess I should have talked to you about it before now, but you won't be too upset that we're splitting up?"

"Nah, mum, you and dad are kind of like freaks being married still. Most of my friends' parents have been divorced for years. It's sort of like our family will be normal now." He gave her an awkward pat on the shoulder. "Anyway, you want a coffee or something? It's getting a bit cold out here. I think I could probably find some clean mugs. Don't know if we've got any milk though."

She followed Ben inside where Faith was just finishing her phone call. "I'm all set," she said. "I called my brother's partner in Invercargill and said I'd be down a few days later than planned."

"We'd better check out the ferry schedule." Anna pulled out her own phone. "We should make some kind of a plan." Her stomach surged, but more with excitement than anxiety. Or vodka.

As they checked their phones to book ferry tickets, Faith's daughter Rachel arrived back from her morning lecture.

"What the bloody hell is that pink van outside?"

"That belongs to me, and to Ben's mum, Anna."

Anna watched as Faith got up and Rachel stooped to hug her much shorter mother. "We're heading off very shortly on a road trip to Uncle Isaac's."

"Well, that's a bit weird but at least we're not having a plumbing emergency. Who'd trust a plumber that turned up in that? It looks a bit dodgy. Why are you going in a crappy old van though?" She shrugged off her jacket and threw it over a chair. "Never mind, I think I'm too hungover to hear about it."

"Rachel!"

"What? You were knocking them back last night before you disappeared. And you look a bit scody yourself mum, if

I'm honest."

Faith sighed and ran her fingers through her hair and Anna wondered whether she was longing for the luxury of her hotel shower as much as she was.

◇

There was a ferry scheduled for later that afternoon, arriving in Picton in the evening. If they left right away they'd make the check-in time. They could then use the time to decide where they'd go from there. And get to know each other a bit better.

"So you want that coffee then?" Ben asked.

The kitchen was covered in glasses and bottles from the night before. A bowl of stale chips sat on the counter and there was guacamole smeared and caked dry on the surface.

"We'd better not. I'm sure we can grab one at the terminal or on the ferry." She gave him a quick kiss.

"What'll I tell Dad if he rings? He was in a right shitty mood before."

As if he'd heard his name, Anna's phone vibrated and she glanced down to see that Greg was calling. Giving Ben and Faith an apologetic look she stepped back out onto the patio.

"Hi," she said resignedly.

"I haven't heard from you. Were you even going to let me know what time you'll be back? You need to pick up my suit from the dry-cleaners," Greg started straight in.

Anna felt her temper rising. "I'm not your bloody slave,

Greg. Get your own dry-cleaning. I'm going down to see the twins and then when I do get back, whenever the hell *that* is, I'm going. This marriage is over."

"The marriage is not over. It's not over until I say it's over," Greg yelled.

"We've been done for a long time. That's been pretty obvious from the fact you've missed all of the counselling sessions except the first one, and now suddenly you're concerned about missing the one today? Well, I'm finally following through. If you don't want to move out I'll pack some stuff when I get back and go."

"And what about the business? Who do you think is going to do invoicing? Huh? You thought about that? You can't just fucking leave me in the lurch."

"Moira can handle it. And if not, she can find someone to help her." Moira did the bulk of the work anyway. She was a capable woman who was probably under-utilised. Anna was only in the office a couple of days a week.

"You're a bloody selfish bitch. Always have been. Do you know how much it's going to cost me to get someone in to clean the house? What are my associates going to think when they find out my wife has just up and left me? Don't be thinking you'll be getting the new cars and fancy clothes and ..."

Anna didn't wait to hear any more. She disconnected and then waved to Faith to indicate she was ready to go.

Chapter three

New Zealand Herald:

PRICELESS ARTIFACT STOLEN FROM TE PAPA

The New Zealand Police are appealing for information from the public to help retrieve a museum piece stolen yesterday from the capital's museum.

The item is believed to be one of Captain James Cook's severed hands, salted and preserved after his death in 1779 when he was executed by Hawaiian natives.

On loan from the United Kingdom, the hand is a rare and irreplaceable piece of history, and is part of a twelve-month display of artifacts for the 250th anniversary of Cook's landing in New Zealand.

Paintings by John Weber and John Cleverly, depicting Cook's final battle and part of the display, were not taken, according to museum curator Safua Akeli Amaama.

The display was due to open this Saturday.

The hand is in a sealed, clear Perspex jar and has a distinctive label declaring it property of the Museum of London.

Police say the piece went missing sometime after closing on Wednesday evening and are following up several leads. They are asking the public for help to locate a person of interest, 27-year-old Gary Harwick, a museum janitor who has not turned up for work since the disappearance.

Faith followed Anna through the crowds of people aboard the ferry, probably off for a weekend away from the capital. Near a large window, a group of women had commandeered two rows of seats. In fact, all the window seats were taken and Anna led her to a row near the front and flopped down. A man a few seats down glanced over at them with disinterest, flipped the page of his newspaper over and then went back to reading. Through the large window at the front Faith could see the wind had picked up, the water was choppy. The engines thrummed through the floor beneath them. She'd never been the best sailor and avoided boats whenever she could. A romantic weekend cruise Daniel had planned for their second wedding anniversary had ended up being a disaster when she spent the entire time heaving her guts out. She'd partly blamed that on the fact that she was pregnant with Rebecca at the time but hadn't been keen to repeat the experience since. She'd never crossed on the ferry before, even though she'd grown up in the South Island. Her parents had never taken her or her brother and sisters outside of their small, conservative community.

"So, what's in Invercargill?" Anna asked.

"My brother lives there. It's his birthday next week and his partner is planning a surprise party to coincide with the opening of their new business." She gazed out the front window and the boat let out a long moaning toot as it started to pull out. "I haven't seen Isaac for years."

"Really? Are you not close then?"

Faith didn't answer for a beat. "We talk, sometimes, on the phone, but no, I guess not. We had a bit of an unconventional childhood, I suppose. I think we're both still coming to terms with that."

Anna turned to face Faith fully. "Sounds interesting. Unconventional how?"

It wasn't something Faith talked about much, and especially with someone she had only just met, but she was going to be spending time with Anna in a small van and their children were flatting together. "Have you heard of the Servants of Christ?"

"Those nutcase Bible-bashers down south? Who don't cut their hair or show any skin above the ankles?"

"Yeah, them. That's where I grew up." Her face quirked into a smile when she saw Anna's mouth drop open.

"Oh God, sorry, that was really insensitive of me ... but, your hair ... it's, like, shoulder length. And, are you allowed to wear jeans?"

"It's okay, I left a long time ago, thank goodness," Faith laughed. "I went to Christchurch to study nursing but I think I was a bit shell-shocked. I did the first year — that's when I met Daniel — we got married, moved up north and had the girls. It wasn't until our youngest, Rebecca, was at school that I went back and studied social work. I think my studies were probably what helped me come to terms with everything in the end. It was kind of cathartic. That and having counselling myself."

"Jesus, I can't imagine what that must have been like," Anna muttered. Then, "God, sorry, can I say 'Jesus' in front of you?"

Faith laughed. "It's fine. I don't belong to the community any more. I'm fully immersed in modern society these days."

"Thank Christ for that, and now I'm going to get us a glass of wine and then you can tell me more."

Anna stood up before Faith could protest. She still felt a bit seedy from the night before, not used to drinking so much.

Faith took the opportunity to call her husband, Daniel, while Anna was gone. He wasn't long home from school, having dropped Rebecca off at volleyball, and was peeling potatoes to make chips for dinner — just a regular Friday night in the Coleman household. He barked out a laugh when Faith told him about the van.

"Ah, that explains things. Rachel was messaging Becky

after school and all Becky could say was 'Oh, my God, Dad, I think Mum's having a mid-life crisis. Should we go down there and rescue her?' I couldn't make out what was going on with all the histrionics."

"What did you say?"

"That it sounded to me like she was trying to get out of doing her biology assignment and she muttered something about the downfalls of having a dad who was a teacher at her school."

"Well, you can reassure her that I'm perfectly fine. I think. It was a moment of drunken madness but it looks like it's all going to work out in the end. Actually, maybe don't mention the drunken madness."

"I won't. I'll tell her you're rediscovering your adventurous side. Actually, I kind of wish I was there to see that for myself. I'm glad you've got someone to travel with though."

"Yeah, I just hope we're not too different. She's very classy. Lots of money. We might not have much other than the kids in common."

"Well, you're great with all types, love, so I'm sure you'll get along fine."

Faith hoped so.

◇

When Anna came back she had an entire bottle of wine, two glasses and a large bowl of loaded wedges.

"I got a Merlot. They didn't have a Malbec, or a Shiraz."

"Oh, I know nothing about wine. If it's red and cheapish, I'll drink it," Faith told her, feeling a little embarrassed at her lack of refinement.

"Well, here's to new friendships," Anna said as she handed Faith a glass.

"So, what about you?" Faith asked, when Anna had sat down and placed the wedges on an empty seat between them. "You have three kids?"

"Yep, the twins are twenty-one this year, both graduating, though I think Niamh is going to go on and do her masters. She's studying business. I'm just glad they're doing what they want to do and are actually going to finish their studies. Unlike me."

Faith was quiet as she waited for Anna to go on.

"I was studying to be a chef when I met Greg. I loved it but he swept me off my feet I guess, at first. It wasn't until we were married that I realised what an arse he was. Wish I'd stayed to finish that final year now, though I wouldn't wish away my kids for anything."

"Do you still love cooking?"

"Absolutely, but now it's just family meals and dinners for Greg's business colleagues. And working part time in our business, that's me." The smile she gave Faith seemed forced.

"So we both feel like we might have missed out a bit then? Perhaps we can have some fun on this trip to make up for it." Faith raised her glass and clinked it against Anna's. "Here's to an amazing adventure."

"Here's to us. By the way, you don't snore, do you?"

"No, do you?"

"No, I don't think so. But if we're going to share a hotel room tonight, I guess you'll find out."

The ferry gave a sudden lurch and Faith sloshed wine over her jeans. It rolled back and she clutched the seat in front to steady herself. Anna reached over for the discarded newspaper the man who had been sitting near them had left behind.

"May as well make ourselves comfy, it could be a bit of a rough trip."

Faith quickly took a couple of wedges, hoping they'd help quell the already queasy feeling she had. She pulled out her phone and sent a quick text to Becky, wishing her a good game and asking how her day at school had been. Becky replied straight away with a sunglasses face emoji and Faith tucked her phone into her pocket, glad Becky was clearly too busy to ask about the road trip. Daniel could explain that one to her later. She really felt quite sick from the rocking to and fro. She sipped her wine as Anna read the paper, humming to herself. Anna stopped suddenly.

"Bloody hell, listen to this. Someone's stolen Captain Cook's hand from Te Papa. Who would want something like that? What would you even do with it?"

"His hand?"

"Yeah, it was part of a display due to open at Te Papa. Sounds like it was quite valuable."

"They must have been hoping to sell it. Don't know how you'd find a buyer for something like that. I wonder what it even looks like?" She let out a shudder. Anna shoved the newspaper in front of her.

"It's pickled. Look, here's a photo."

Faith looked. She couldn't not. The hand was in a clear tube, swimming in liquid. It was withered, the skin wrinkled, the fingers claw-like. Absolutely gruesome – like something that would reach out to grab you in your worst nightmare. Her stomach lurched. She quickly shoved her glass of wine at Anna, clapped her hand over her mouth and stumbled to the outside door as quickly as she could.

◇

Anna looked at her sympathetically when she returned. "I got you some water," she said, handing Faith a bottle. "The guy at the till says it's those southwesterlies that cause the swell but luckily they don't get that many of them. Well, unlucky for us, I guess, that we got one today. Is there anything I can do to help?"

"Distract me?" Faith suggested, twisting off the top and taking a large mouthful.

"So where do you live? I can't remember whether you've said."

"We're in the Hawke's Bay, quite near where Daniel grew up. His parents have been an amazing support to both of us over the years and they adore the girls."

"Rachel looks nothing like you. Does she take after your husband?"

"Daniel. Yeah, she does. Rebecca is more like me. We're all shorties in my family." She pulled up a photo on her phone and turned it to show Anna. Daniel was lounging on a hammock in their backyard, asleep, with a book over his chest. His sunglasses were skewed, one hand rested on the slight paunch of his stomach and his feet were bare, hanging over the edge. Rebecca sat on the grass nearby, hair the same dark brown as Faith's, her round face split into a wide grin.

"Do you have any photos? Ben looks very much like you, I think."

"Here, this was Greg and me at an awards dinner last year."

Faith peered at the photo showing a very glamorous couple. Greg was a dark-haired man wearing a well-fitting charcoal suit, an expensive-looking watch peeking out from the perfectly turned cuff. He was good-looking in a bland, unremarkable way, looking directly into the camera with an unreadable smirk on his face. Next to him, Anna looked poised and elegant in a long silver dress with a plunging neckline, one hand placed demurely across her cleavage. Her blonde hair was swept up into a neat chignon and her makeup looked flawless.

"Oh wow, you look stunning. I couldn't even imagine pulling off something like that."

Anna giggled. "Want to hear a funny story? I spent all night trying to stop my boobs from popping out of the neckline. I just felt so self-conscious the whole time. It wasn't until we got home that I realised I'd put the dress on the wrong way. The plunge was meant to be at the back."

Faith snorted. "Well, you'd never know it to look at you. You ooze confidence."

"I'm just glad Greg didn't win the bloody award. Every year he gets nominated and he's convinced each time that this is going to be the year he's going to win. Of course, I'd have had to go up with him to accept it like his little show pony. Imagine how mortified I'd have been afterwards when I'd realised."

The ferry rose suddenly and then dropped and Faith felt her stomach roll in response. She grimaced, and handed her glass to Anna again as she stood. "Sorry," she muttered as she pushed her way to the bathroom.

◇

"That has to be one of the worst sailings I've had in all the years I've worked here," Janice told Faith as she handed her another paper towel in the ladies before they disembarked. "Sometimes those rough sailings just come out of the blue."

Anna had seemed mostly unaffected by the swells, but Faith had spent a large amount of the journey in the stall and had gotten to know Janice quite well as they sailed. As Janice bagged up yet another bin of rubbish, another woman emerged from the far stall looking as green as Faith felt.

"I think I've lost about five kgs in the last two hours," the woman said.

"Hopefully the trip back will be better," Janice said cheerfully, and Faith shuddered at the thought.

"Right, well, thanks for your help, Janice, and good luck with the surgery," she said.

"Enjoy your road trip, love, I'm sure you'll have a great time."

Faith hoped so. Getting off the ferry would make a great start.

Chapter four

Picton was beautiful as they sailed into its harbour and eventually disembarked. The sun was low in the sky creating a stunning backdrop against the sea edge. There was no sign of the bad weather that had caused the crossing to be so rough.

They both held their breath as Anna turned the key to the van, but it started fine. Anna gave the dash a gentle pat.

"We should give her a name," Faith said as they drove slowly down the line to exit.

"Hmmm, maybe Rizzo? Wasn't she a Pink Lady? I can't actually remember any of the others."

"What's a Pink Lady?" Faith asked.

"You know, *Grease*?"

Faith must have looked blank because Anna looked shocked.

"The movie? Don't tell me you've never seen *Grease*?"

"Sheltered upbringing, remember," Faith said with a laugh.

"Oh man, we have to watch it sometime, it's a classic." Anna gave her a rundown of the general plot as they drove to find a petrol station.

"... And then Sandy turns up, transformed into a bad girl in leathers, with a cigarette ..." Anna paused. "Man, this movie hasn't aged well, now that I think about it."

They pulled up next to a gas pump and both got out.

"I'll pump the gas and you get snacks?" Anna offered.

"Sounds good." Faith wandered into the building and gathered up some chips and drinks and then dawdled a while at the candy section before she joined Anna at the counter. She was looking stressed, fumbling in her bag.

"Everything okay?" Faith asked.

"My bloody card isn't working," Anna told her. She handed over a black Visa to the attendant.

"Can I try this one instead? Sorry."

They waited while the lady re-entered the amount but that card was declined as well.

"That fucking prick," Anna said under her breath. "He's cut off my bloody cards."

"I can get it," Faith said, doing a quick calculation in her head. She thought there was just enough in her account.

"Sorry," Anna told her. She seemed embarrassed.

"Don't stress, I've had my card decline on me plenty of times."

They jumped back into the van and Anna started the engine. Then turned it off and turned to face Faith.

"Shit. What do we do now? I was going to pay the hotel but it looks like I need to get to a bank first and sort out new cards. God, Greg's a dick."

"Well, I don't think I have enough for a hotel, sorry," Faith said, looking in her purse. "How much cash do you have?"

They sat and pooled their money into the centre console. Between them they had ninety-three dollars and seventy cents.

"Well, I think we need to be very frugal," Faith said. "Perhaps a backpackers?"

"Yeah but we'll need more gas and food too." Anna looked over her shoulder and into the back of the van. "I guess we could always sleep in Rizzo?" she said dubiously.

They sat looking at the thin beds for a beat.

"How bad can it be, right?" Faith said, trying not to think about how clean the bedding might be. Or not be, more likely.

"And it's only till we get to Christchurch," Anna agreed.

"Right then, it's settled. We'll sleep in the back and it'll be part of the adventure."

Anna started up the engine again.

"Shall we just get going and drive till we find somewhere to park up?"

"Yeah, I guess, no point hanging around in Picton is there?"

They set off, returning to the topic of T-Birds and John

Travolta, and Faith felt quite cheerful, like this was going to be okay after all.

They shared a bag of chips as they drove and chatted for a bit about their kids.

"What did your husband say about all this?" Anna asked.

"Oh, he was fine. He's not expecting me back until next week anyway and he and Becky get on well. They have a good system going. And she's very independent. It's lovely when your kids get bigger and don't need you as much in some ways, isn't it?"

"Yes, but then sometimes I miss the days when they were little, and so lovely, you know?"

"True. I did love those days at home with mine when they thought you were their world."

"Still, it was nice when they went to school and you could breathe again."

"Very true," Faith agreed.

"So, why social work?" Anna asked.

"I think I just really like helping people. I love my job. And maybe my upbringing being so out of the norm made it easier for me to see things from different perspectives? I enjoy the challenge of making a difference, and helping people help themselves, I guess."

"That's so great. I bet you're bloody good at your job."

"Aw, thanks."

They were both feeling a bit weary and Faith couldn't stop

yawning. She fiddled with the radio a bit but just got static. There was only the awful rap CD in the slot to listen to.

"I bet Barney is bummed he left his *Chillinit* CD behind," Faith said with a grin. She opened the glove box to check if there were any other finds. There was a very mangled up owner's manual, a pack of rolling papers and an old pair of scratched-up sunglasses. Faith pulled them out and noticed the corner of a plastic bag sticking up under the manual. She gave it a tug, pulling out a resealable bag full of what looked to her to be grass clippings.

"What on the earth?" She held it up. "What is this?"

Anna looked over at her and shrieked, the van swerving momentarily into the other lane, and then she pulled over to the side of the road, churning up gravel as she braked.

"Oh, my God, that's *drugs*!" Anna said. Faith let go of the bag and it dropped onto the gearbox.

"What? But I've touched it. My fingerprints will be all over it."

Anna picked it up, and inspected it.

"It looks like pot." She sniffed the outside, then pulled open the seal to inspect the contents. The skunky scent of musk hit them straight away.

"Bloody hell," Anna said. "That's definitely pot. I bet Barney wishes he'd remembered to get that."

"Well, what do we *do* with it?" Faith asked. She was feeling a bit panicked and she probably sounded dramatic, but she'd never been around marijuana before.

"I don't know. We need to get rid of it somehow. Put it back for now though," Anna said, passing it to her. Faith took one corner gingerly between her finger and her thumb and then placed it gently back in the glove box, clicking it closed like it contained an undetonated bomb.

"I didn't even vote yes in the referendum," she said.

"Hey, look," Anna said and Faith looked up at where she was pointing. About five metres in front of them was a sign illuminated by the van's headlights that read 'Cox Creek Campsite 100m'.

Although they hadn't gone far, it was getting dark and it seemed like a good idea to stop, so they rattled down the path to find a compact container office. To one side was a small ablution block, and there were six camp plots along the water's edge, divided at one point by a grassy area with a picnic table and a barbecue. One site had a Jucy camper van parked in it, another had a small two-man tent.

There was no sign of anyone around. Faith got out and found a note attached to the flimsy door, asking anyone arriving after 5pm and before 7am to pay the $15 fee into the honesty box. She found the cash and posted it through the thin slot.

Anna drove up and parked next to the other van. They could hear soft music coming from inside it. Trees lined the lake's bank and the smell of pine needles filled the air as they hopped out of the van and stretched.

"Right then," Faith said. "Now what?"

Anna pulled the almost full bottle of wine out from her Coach tote.

"Let's have a drink," she said. "And then we need to get rid of that bag of weed."

Chapter five

Picton News:

TOURISTS GIVEN WARNING AFTER INDECENT EXPOSURE

A couple have been let off with a warning after police were called to a South Island campground amid numerous complaints from locals.

The couple, on holiday from Sweden, were seen engaging in various sex acts at a DOC campground on Wednesday in full view of the other holidaymakers.

"They were definitely dogging," said Mr Larson, who was staying with his wife in the encampment.

Under the 1961 Crimes Act, public nudity and sex in a public place is an illegal offence, but when questioned the pair claimed not to be aware they were doing anything wrong and no charges were laid.

Faith cracked open the van doors and Anna scrummaged in the plastic box to see if there were any glasses. She found a metal mug and used the top of a thermos to pour them both a drink. They sat at the picnic table and looked out at the river. It was close to a full moon and it's light illuminated the water.

"Gosh, this is lovely," Faith said with a sigh.

"It is, isn't it?"

It really was. Despite the fact that Anna was fuming over Greg cancelling her credit cards, she was actually enjoying herself. Faith seemed lovely, and she was glad to be out of Auckland and looking forward to seeing the twins.

They sat in silence for a bit, enjoying the quiet.

"There's baked beans in the box," Anna said after a while, "and pots and things. We could heat some of those up for dinner."

"Yeah, okay. I wonder if there are showers?" Faith said. "I feel a bit gross."

"We could always have a swim in the morning. That water looks gorgeous."

"It is, ve have been in zere earlier," a man said from behind them, making Anna lurch against Faith in surprise, clutching her mug to avoid spilling her wine.

They both turned to find an older couple standing behind them, both with long grey hair in ponytails and wearing identical tie-dyed harem pants.

"Jesus, you scared the shite out of me," Anna said.

"Ve thought ve might join you for a drink." The woman held up a bottle of wine. "I am Helene and this is Klaus," she said as she sat across from Faith.

"Ve 'ave sausages." Klaus held out a large package of sausages like an offering. "Zere is a fire. Everybody likes a nice sausage, ya?" He winked in their direction, or perhaps Anna was imagining that and he just had something in his eye. While Helene poured wine for herself and Klaus, Anna fossicked around in the van and found the baked beans, a small pot and a can opener.

"... the ranger, he is not a nice person, how you say, intolerant," Helene was saying to Faith when she returned. "Last night he came by late while Klaus and I were enjoying ourselves very much by the river and told us ve should be not in public and to return to our van."

"Like a curfew? I've never heard of that before," Faith said. "That doesn't sound right. He sounds a bit power-hungry."

"He said he would call ze police. Ve vere not 'arming anyone. Zere was nobody around. Ve vere sure to check zis time."

◇

The barbecue was more of a simple fire pit with a grill. Luckily someone had left wood and pine cones in a neat pile next to it and Klaus quickly got it lit and, once it had died down to an acceptable level, started to cook the sausages. Anna took the beans over and tipped them into the pot. She couldn't remember the last time she'd had such a simple meal, but washed down with a couple of glasses of wine it wasn't too bad. Greg would have turned his nose up if she'd cooked sausages for dinner. It reminded her of when she'd been camping with her parents and brothers as a child. She and Greg had never done camping trips with the kids and she regretted that now. She felt they'd missed out.

When they'd finished eating, Helene filled a large pot with water and put it on the fire to heat up for the dishes.

"Only cold water in ze showers, I can heat more if you want to take your clothes off and wash in ze warm," she said.

"I don't think I'll bother tonight. It's getting a bit chilly." Faith had her arms wrapped around herself. "I'm going to get my cardigan from the van – do you want me to grab you something, Anna?"

"Yeah, thanks, I have a jumper in my bag. It should be on top, a grey one."

"If you are cold at the night, our van is very warm. A foursome of bodies would produce a nice heat," Klaus said. He threw another couple of pieces of wood onto the fire and waggled his eyebrows suggestively.

Anna turned the choking sound that came out into a cough. When Faith came back she pulled her jumper on. It was angora, way too nice to be sitting in front of a fire really.

"You ladies, you are not sisters? You are together?" Helene indicated between Anna and Faith.

"Yes, we're together, not sisters."

"Not together, together. We're just friends," Anna clarified.

"We're still getting to know each other. We're on a bit of a journey of discovery," Faith beamed.

"A road trip," Anna told them hastily. She drained the last of the bottle into their glasses and gave a loud fake yawn. "Must be almost bedtime. I get very ornery if I don't get enough sleep."

Klaus drained his glass and he and Helene stood. "You know vere ve are if you do feel 'orny. You are velcome to join us, either of you. Or both." He winked again. It was definitely a wink this time and they headed for their van, leaving Anna gaping.

"Oh God, I said ornery, as in grumpy, not bloody horny."

"I thought it was just me. They were kind of giving off weird vibes, weren't they?"

"Maybe it's just the language difference? Hopefully."

There was the crunch of tyres on gravel and headlights illuminated the campsite as a car swung around the bend in the driveway.

"Oh gosh. Is that the ranger?" Faith asked.

"Shit, the weed. What if he finds it and calls the police?" Anna went to jump up but Faith was already on her feet and halfway to the van. She returned, waving the bag of marijuana, not very discreetly, eyes wide with panic. The car came to a halt nearby.

"Oh heck, I don't want to go to jail." Faith flung the bag onto the embers of the fire. There was a faint sizzle and a pungent smell of burning plastic, and then an earthy, herbal aroma filled the air.

The car door opened and two people got out. "Evening," someone called, and then they heard the sound of the tent unzipping.

Faith breathed in deeply, huffed out as though relieved and then giggled. "It's just the campers. At least if the ranger comes we've got rid of the ..." She leant towards Anna and whispered dramatically, "... paraphernalia."

"When you think about it though, what would a ranger have done? It's not like he'd have authority to search the van, is it? We probably overreacted." A breeze blew smoke from the barbecue directly into her face and she coughed, then picked up her mug, holding it towards Faith in a toast. "Cheers, here's to getting to know each other."

"And not in a biblical way," Faith added, causing Anna to almost choke on her wine.

They sat silently for a bit, enjoying the last of their drinks, listening to the faint sound of the river and the near silence of the night. Despite the slight temperature drop it was still lovely out. A morepork hooted nearby, out on the hunt for its evening meal.

"I'm glad I don't have to eat mice," Faith said suddenly.

That sounded very profound to Anna. She nodded in agreement. Her head felt heavy and she was suddenly not sure that she was nodding at all so she put her hand up to feel whether her head was moving or not. It didn't seem to be.

"Do you think the stars are looking at us?" she said.

"They are. With their shiny little faces."

"Shiny happy faces. Or is it shiny happy people?"

"I think my feet are numb. Anna, can you have a look and see if my feet are numb?"

Anna had flopped back onto the grass and now heaved herself into a sitting position. "Faith? I think maybe we're just a teeny bit high."

"High on life?"

"No, high on the weed you just burnt."

"Wow. I've never been high before." Faith stood and spread her arms as wide as they could go. "I think I like it. We should go for a swim."

"You're nuts, it'll be freezing. Anyway, I don't have any togs," Anna replied stupidly.

"I don't have nuts," Faith said earnestly, making Anna laugh loudly. "Anyway, who needs togs?" Faith had started to throw her clothes off. Her shirt narrowly missed the still-glowing barbecue. "I've also never been skinny-dipping before."

Anna felt suddenly drained. She had an odd sensation that she was both floating and grounded. "I need to go to bed," she said, heaving herself up with some difficulty.

"I'm just going to dunk myself in the water first. It will be my un-baptism."

"Do you think I should watch you to make sure you don't drown?"

"It'll be fine. My sisters and I used to swim in the river at home in full-length dresses and enormous flannel bloomers. We were the epitome of modesty."

Anna made her way to the van, fumbling around until she found the door to the back. She had no idea whether there was a light anywhere so she groped around until she found one of the narrow beds, feeling her way up it and then quickly stripped off her jeans and slid under the musty duvet. Her elbow whacked the wall as she shuffled about trying to get comfortable. The bed was lumpy and she was glad she was too drunk and stoned to think about what the bedding might contain. Although, now that she'd thought about it ...

◇

There was a sudden clatter, jolting Anna from her state of almost-sleep. The back door of the van was flung open and Faith stumbled inside, the moon at her back illuminating her. She was clutching her clothes in a heap to her chest and breathing rapidly as though she'd just swum an entire leg of a triathlon. Anna raised her head and looked blearily at her.

"Holy cow, we weren't imagining things," Faith said. "Which bed am I in?"

She patted her way around, found her bag and pulled something out of it, seemed to establish which bed she was sleeping in and then pulled the door shut. They were plunged into darkness again and Anna heard Faith shuffling about as she got settled.

"I went for my swim – it was so nice, by the way, you should go in the morning – and then I got a bit mixed up and I got into the wrong van."

"What wrong van?"

"Klaus and Helene's. I got into their van by mistake. I was standing there, stark naked, and Helene said," – Faith put on an accent that sounded remarkably like Helene – "'Ahh, you do vant ze meat and two vag.'"

"Two vag? She did not."

"I swear, she did. I don't think it was a language thing either. I didn't know what to say so I just got out of there. Oh my gosh, we're going to have to leave before the sun is up. I'm so embarrassed."

Anna let her head fall back onto the pillow. She started to giggle. Faith joined in and soon they were laughing so hard she was sure Rizzo must be rocking from the outside. Anna had to get up to pee in a very undignified manner in the grass on the other side of the van and then they finally settled down to go to sleep.

"'Night, Faith," she said, once she'd finally stopped snorting.

"'Night, Anna. At least these beds are more comfy than they look."

"You must still be completely out of it," Anna told her.

Chapter six

Anna woke up feeling like she'd slept on a bed of nails. Faith, however, claimed her bed was great but she couldn't help feeling a bit precious, like the lead in the *Princess and the Pea* story.

When they stumbled out of the van, it was to the most unpleasant sight. Klaus and Helene were having a rather bendy, noisy shag in front of the now-cold fire pit, his pale naked arse rising and then falling with a loud slap. They tried clearing their throats and banging around to make the couple realise they were up, but it didn't seem to deter them. If anything, it may have spurred them on.

When Anna saw Klaus wielding one of the very charred sausages left on the barbecue, she decided it was time to move on.

They stopped at the toilet block to have a quick, shockingly cold shower and brush their teeth. Anna ran a brush through her long hair and looked around futilely for somewhere to plug in her hairdryer. There were no outlets. She groaned inwardly. Her hair would frizz up without a good blow-wave and become unruly. Still, she supposed it didn't really matter, but she was used to drying it and it felt odd to leave it wet.

She'd only packed for two nights in Wellington, so she was running very low on clean clothes. Putting on her last clean pair of knickers, she was quietly glad that she always overpacked a little. She bypassed her Karen Walker top as being a little nice for a trip on the road and did a sniff test of her other tops to find the cleanest one. She'd need to either do some laundry or buy something else to wear — once she got her finances sorted.

The fact that Greg had been such a jerk and had cut off her card was infuriating. She was going to have to talk to a lawyer when she got back to Auckland. She'd left things too long, worrying about the kids, and feeling like she owed it to them to put up with an unhappy marriage.

They hit the road, breaking open a packet of biscuits for breakfast.

"I'm dying for a coffee," she told Faith as they pulled out onto the main road.

"I'm mostly a herbal tea girl myself, " Faith told her. "Unless I've been drinking. Then it's Earl Grey. We weren't allowed coffee growing up, just herbal tea, and try as I might to like it, I just don't. Unless it's a mocha, I guess. I love chai now though."

"Okay, so tell me if I'm being too nosy, but what was it like growing up in a place like that?"

Faith unscrewed the top and passed her a bottle of water.

"In a lot of ways, it was good, you know? Lots of fresh air and nature, and other kids. No television, but we didn't know to miss that. But, we had a lot of chores. And there's a lot of praying. A lot of indoctrination. It's a funny thing. You're expected to just believe what you're told is God's will for you, no questions asked." Faith drank her own water and took another biscuit before she continued. "We had to do a lot of cooking and a lot of laundry. I liked it a lot better when we got bigger and had to attend mainstream school."

"So how many kids are there in your family?"

"Five, including me — three sisters and a brother. My parents would have had more, but Mother had complications with me and had to have medical intervention and a hysterectomy."

"Oh, so did your dad get another wife?"

"No, they don't do polygamy. Probably only because the community is too small."

"So, what are your siblings' names?"

"There's Isaac, he's the oldest, and he's turning fifty next week. Then Grace, who's married with five kids, Charity who's forty-three, I think, and Hope who has four kids. Isaac and I are the only ones who left the commune. So then there's me, and I just turned forty." Faith pulled a face. "How old are you?"

"Forty-four," Anna told her. "So what made you leave? Was it your husband? Ohh, are you, like, banned? You know how like no one can talk to you if you leave the Amish?"

"Excommunicated, you mean? No, not really, but my parents were very unhappy with me, and I haven't seen them since Daniel and I got married." The van made a weird grinding noise as they went round a windy corner and they both paused nervously to see if it did it again. It stayed quiet, so Faith continued.

"I somehow convinced my parents to let me do nursing. A school friend was going and she and I went together to Christchurch and stayed in the nurses homes. Which is where I met Daniel."

"Was he doing nursing too?"

"No, teachers college, but he was going out with another girl on our floor until he met me."

"Aww, cute."

"I suppose so. Anyway, I struggled through my first year, and Daniel finished his training and then I got pregnant."

Anna gave Faith a look. "Ohhhh. Shit."

"Yeah, my parents were *not* happy. We got married, but of course they had imagined I was behaving myself and would come back to be a nurse in their community and marry a follower."

"Still, all these years later, and two kids? You'd think they'd have gotten over it?"

Faith sighed. "You don't know my father. He's staunch. To him, sin is sin."

They spotted a small bakery with a footpath sign advertising coffees and Anna pulled the van up outside. There were no tables so they sat back in the cab to eat their Danish and drink their hot drinks.

"I feel bad that you're doing all the driving," Faith said. "But I only learnt to drive after I got married and had the kids, and we never had a manual. I could try though?"

"Nah, it's fine," Anna told her. I grew up on a farm, so I can drive most things. I'm kind of enjoying it actually."

"Do you live on a farm now? In Auckland?"

Anna laughed. "Hell, no. Greg is no farmer. He wouldn't know a ewe from a ram. No, we're on the North Shore and so is the packaging company we own. It's all in the city."

"Oh, sounds ... interesting," Faith said unconvincingly.

Anna laughed again. "No, it's really not. I wish I'd never dropped out of my studies."

"So we're both dropouts then," Faith said.

They both smiled.

"Yeah but you went back and did something else later. I didn't."

"You still could."

"Maybe." Anna realised she would have to think about what she would do when she got back. She'd be out of a job, after all. And she didn't want to do office work.

"So, what else do we have in common, I wonder?" Faith

said.

"Well, tell me something else about you. Hobbies? Weird habits? Favourite book?"

"Oh, the Bible for sure," Faith said and then cracked up at the horrified look on Anna's face.

◇

They spent the rest of the drive to Christchurch chatting and getting to know each other better. When they got to the city, Anna googled the nearest bank and parked outside. The van made another strange grinding noise as they stopped.

The bank was closed. It was Saturday and Anna hadn't even considered they wouldn't be open.

"Shit. I've lost track of days. We'll have to stay till Monday to sort things."

"Oh well, I assumed we'd be here at least one night anyway. I don't think it'll make too much difference."

"No, I suppose not, but it means another few nights sleeping in the van."

Faith looked happy enough at the prospect and Anna steeled herself not to be such a diva, but she wasn't looking forward to more nights on the lumpy mattress.

It was a mindset thing, she realised. As a kid, she and her brothers had loved camping out on the farm, swimming in the river and getting grubby. What had changed? She wasn't that old. She needed to find the old her who would have found it an adventure.

Chapter seven

They were both starving, but low on cash, so they drove to a cheap burger place. Anna tried not to think about her yoga instructor's disapproving face as she ate.

"I'm sorry I can't afford to contribute more money," Faith said. She seemed embarrassed. "I was planning on staying with my brother, and we don't have a lot of spare cash at the moment with me only working part time."

"Oh, no. It's fine," Anna reassured her. "Honestly, at least we're doing something a bit different. Greg would never do anything like this. His idea of the perfect holiday is the same every year. Ten days in Hawaii, golf, shopping and drinks. It's nice to do something out of my comfort zone."

"Well, that doesn't sound awful, but I see your point." Faith took a gulp of her drink and then hiccupped. "We can pretend we're teenagers again and do all the things we never did." She sounded a bit wistful, Anna thought.

"Well, what else shall we do then? What didn't you do that you wish you had? Tattoo? Piercing? Streak across a rugby field? We could do a bucket list."

Faith laughed. "I would actually love to get my ears pierced. I wasn't allowed as a kid. But that's a bit tame, isn't it?"

"Well, you had your chance for a totally wild night last night," Anna said with a laugh. Faith threw her burger wrapper at her. "Don't, I'm mortified just thinking about it!"

"Speaking of which, I think I might have to see if one of the kids can lend me some money," Anna said, pulling out her phone. "But I've just realised they don't even know I'm coming. So I'd better give them a heads-up so they can get rid of any overnight guests and clean up a bit. Hopefully I can use their washing machine too. I need some clean clothes."

"We passed a thrift store on the way here," Faith said. "If you really want to relive your youth we could always have a dig around there to pass some time."

"Oh, yes, I used to love a good vintage shop hunt. I once found a Louis Vuitton handbag in one in Hamilton when I was at tech."

◇

The thrift store was less 'bargain finds' and more 'dead people cast-offs'. It smelt like a mouldy rest home. Long piles of shoes under the clothes rack made Anna nauseous at the thought of all the toe jam and bunions. She was not a fan of feet.

She skipped the swimwear and underwear tables and

flicked through a rack of tops, looking for something that would fit her, and didn't have dubious stains.

Faith was looking at the kitchenware on a long shelf at the back wall.

"Oh man, they have a fondue set. I've always wanted to have a fondue. And it's only twelve dollars."

"Well, I think I only need a top and maybe some leggings to tide me over, and they have two for ten dollar T-shirts so we may have enough? We could do that tonight."

Faith wandered over to search the T-shirt rack with her.

"Oh, my God, look, a *Baywatch* T-shirt," Anna said with a laugh. "I always wanted to be Pamela Anderson."

"Who?"

Anna showed her the top. It featured a pair of large, enhanced breasts in a skimpy, red, one-piece swimming costume. When she held it up, it moulded to her torso to look as if they were hers.

"Pammy. She was the hot lifeguard in an old TV show when I was young. Man, we need to do a movie marathon sometime to get you up to date with all the nineties TV you missed out on."

"That top is hilarious. Although your boobs are just as impressive."

"Well, thank you," Anna said, putting the top back.

"You should get it," Faith said. "I bet teenaged you would have."

Anna laughed. Then she pulled a black T-shirt from the

rack.

“I will if you get this.” The T-shirt featured an outline of a long-haired man on a cross, one hand holding a ghetto blaster. The words ‘JESUS IS MY HOMEBOY’ were written across the top.

“Deal,” Faith said with a grin.

◇

Cameron and Niamh lived in Riccarton near the university so they drove out to their place and pulled up into the driveway. Greg and Anna had purchased the flat in their second year down there as an investment. It was a three-bedroom place. Greg had assumed that Ben would also study there and had not been happy when he chose Wellington instead. But the twins had rented the third bedroom out, and that money covered most of their living expenses.

The place smelt of lemon and pine like it had been freshly cleaned. Cameron was home but about to go to work at his bar job and told her that Niamh was at the uni library but would be back at six. Their flatmate was also heading out and Anna couldn’t remember his name. He was a drummer in a band with a long goatee and a handlebar moustache. He gave both her and Faith a kiss on the cheek as he left and then Cameron as well. Anna raised her eyebrows at her son. He grinned and shook his head.

“Just friends, Mum, he’s not my type.”

“You have a type?” Anna laughed as she hugged him.

"This is Faith, her daughter Rachel is flatting with Ben."

"Hi, Faith." He shook Faith's hand. He was tall and lanky, with shoulder-length dark hair, thick brows and warm amber-coloured eyes. He had several piercings in one ear and an expander in his lobe.

"So, what's going on with Dad?' he asked Anna. "He rang and had a mental about some awards thing and you taking off."

"Well, I don't want to just drop it on you, but I'm going to move out when I get home, hun," Anna told him.

"Okay," he shrugged. Anna watched his face for a reaction. He seemed unfazed.

"How do you feel about that?" she asked, picking at a cuticle.

"Well, I'm not surprised really," he told her. "We've been expecting it." He gave her a small smile. "Don't worry about us, Mum, we're adults. And if you're happier apart, I get it."

"Thanks, sweetheart," Anna said, trying not to cry. Cameron did a little laugh and gave her a long hug. He was so tall and she realised she hadn't hugged him in a while. He always seemed bigger than she was expecting. She remembered the days when he would climb into her lap to hug her and laughed at the thought of him doing that now. He pulled away first and they wandered into the lounge.

"What time are you working till?" Anna asked.

"Saturday night, so probably around two." He looked at his phone. "Actually I better get going. Where are you staying?"

"Oh, this will crack you up," Anna said. "Check out our wheels on your way out."

He gave her a bemused look.

"Okay, so I'll see you tomorrow sometime then?"

"We'll be right on your doorstep when you wake up," Anna said with a grin. "Now, before you go, have you got any wine? Or money? I'm skint. I'll pay you back."

"Mum," he laughed, "literally no one says 'skint'." He didn't even ask why she had no money on her, perhaps because Faith was there, Anna guessed. Or Greg had been boasting about cutting her off. He pulled out his wallet and gave her five twenties.

"I think there's an open bottle of Pinot in the fridge," he said, "or there's a bottle of gin in the pantry. Enjoy."

Chapter eight

The *Press*:

STUDENT SIT-IN ENDS IN BLOODBATH

A peaceful protest by the Christchurch Vegetarian Society turned violent after one member threw blood on supermarket workers in Riccarton early yesterday evening.

A person in their early twenties was removed by police after they swilled supermarket butchery employees with pig's blood. They are expected to face several charges.

Mila Towbridge, the society president, said the incident had not been planned and no one else was aware of the intended action.

The supermarket was closed overnight for cleaning. The owner, Alan Jones, said he'd "had a gutsful of all these bleeding heart liberals."

Meat consumption in New Zealand has reduced greatly in the past few years with 31% of the population now eating less or no meat while only 3% are full vegan.

Faith had purchased the fondue set in the end so after Anna put on some washing, including the bedding from Rizzo, they decided to wander down to the local supermarket and get some cheese and bits and pieces to cook in it.

When they got there, there was a crowd of people outside with placards.

A middle-aged woman wearing overalls and Doc Martens was shouting into a megaphone "*Meat is murder!*" A harassed-looking man in tan slacks with the beginnings of a comb-over was talking animatedly with several supermarket staff, gesturing wildly at the protesters. His name badge said 'Alan'.

"My apologies, ladies, please, please, let them through," he said, waving his arms wildly to try to create a space to the store entrance. Anna and Faith slipped in, and then had a small struggle with a young dreadlocked woman over the shopping baskets.

"Tell me you won't be putting dead animals in here," she said, gripping one handle.

Faith tugged gently on the other handle. "Well, I was thinking just a little bit of steak, or maybe some meatballs?"

"You can't," the woman implored them. "Think of those poor calves, ripped from their mothers, those sad, beautiful eyes."

Faith did love cows. She looked over at Anna, who rolled her eyes a little.

"Well, yes, it's very sad, but I mean, they're already dead, aren't they?" Anna said. "And we're designed to eat meat after all."

They'd given up getting the basket from the woman and she was trailing along with them down the aisle, talking about the impact of effluent on the waterways and sustainable crop harvesting as Anna put various things into the basket that they were still holding awkwardly between them.

"Look, hun, I appreciate what you're trying to do. I just don't think this is the best way to go about it," Faith told her.

The girl looked furtively around the store and then leant in to whisper.

"To be honest, I love animals, but I'm really here about the owner," she said in a hushed whisper. "He's an arsehole. My sister used to work here and he was always making gross comments and 'accidentally' brushing up against her and stuff. He does it to all the new girls."

"Really?" Faith said. "Has anyone reported him?"

"Yeah, but so far no one has had enough proof. Their word against his. So I figure I'll get him where it hurts, stuff up his business."

"Who is this guy?" Anna asked, and the woman – her name was Jen, she told them – pointed to Alan still in the front entrance. They could see him through the automatic doors, talking to one of the young girls in a supermarket uniform and as if on cue, he gave her a hug, his meaty hand slipping down to cup her bottom. She jumped back and he gave her a leery grin.

"Eww, what a creep," Faith said. "I've half a mind to join you."

"We're going to do a sit-in in ten minutes or so," Jen said. "The more people the better."

Faith looked at Anna, who was still watching the front doorway. She turned to look at Faith and grinned.

"A sit-in, eh? That's exactly what I would have done in my youth. Shall we?"

"Really?" Faith said. Half of her wanted to do it, just to say she had, and it might be quite exciting. The other half, the responsible one, was thinking that it was a bit silly to get involved. And she was looking forward to the fondue and a glass of wine. But Jen was looking imploringly at her, and Alan was definitely trying to look down the girl's top now, and ...

"To heck with it. Let's do it," she said.

◇

A sit-in, it transpired, wasn't really very thrilling. Just boring. They were camped out in front of the meat chillers and it was very draughty. The metallic smell of meat was a bit gross, and Faith had been stuck talking to an earnest young guy called Flax for the last fifteen minutes about the merits of lentils versus tofu.

Anna nudged her shoulder. "Hey, how long do these things take anyway?"

"I don't know," Faith confessed, "but I'm starving." She eyed the cheese and bread in their shopping basket.

"Me too, and my arms are tired from holding this thing up." Anna's neighbouring protester Judy had given her a large sign with the words 'IT'S NOT FOOD, IT'S VIOLENCE'.

"I don't know if it's all the talk about meat, and maybe I'm just imagining it, but I swear I can smell pies," Faith said, her stomach grumbling.

"No, I can smell it too," Anna said. She put the sign up and did an exaggerated stretch. "I just need to take a toilet break," she said to the others. "Faith, did you want to go too?" She gave her a wink.

Faith jumped to her feet, the shopping basket in one hand.

"Yes, yes, we'll be right back," she said to Flax, moving off towards the checkouts.

Around the corner, they found a middle-aged woman in a floral apron handing out sausage roll samples to the other shoppers.

"Would you care to try one of our new pork, apple and fennel rolls?" she asked Faith, holding out one on a napkin.

"Oh yes, that sounds lovely," Faith said and she and Anna stood eating their rolls with contented murmurs until the woman offered them seconds.

Unfortunately that was where Judy and Flax found them.

They were less than impressed. A small argument ensued where they were called traitors, turncoats and deserters and Faith was relieved when the police came in the store entrance, and Judy tugged Flax back to link arms with the others. She and Anna whipped through the self-checkout and shot out into the car park just as a woman in a cow suit passed them, carefully carrying a large red bucket.

◇

Back at the flat, Faith met Niamh, who was a doppelganger for her mother with her long legs, blonde hair and open cheerful face. They set to work making the fondue and pouring glasses of wine.

"Is that hideous pink thing really what you guys are driving?" Niamh asked as she carefully skewered a piece of pear onto her fondue fork.

"Yep. That's Rizzo," Anna said.

"My God, that's a far cry from your usual transportation, Mum. It's nothing like your Land Rover, is it?" Anna grinned and gave her daughter the finger.

Faith shoved a cheesy mouthful of bread into her mouth and watched Anna. They obviously were very well off, yet Anna didn't seem at all snooty or pretentious. Her phone chimed a text and she saw it was Daniel, just checking in.

"I might just ring home if you don't mind?" she told the others, taking her wine glass and heading into the lounge. Daniel answered on the second ring.

"Hey, babe. How's the intrepid journey going?"

"Good, we're in Christchurch now. Going to head off Monday after we go to the bank." Faith gave him a quick rundown on the situation, conscious not to say too much in case they could hear her from the dining room.

"Did you sleep in the van then?" he asked.

"We did. Although I almost ended up in a ménage à trois first," Faith said with a laugh. "I'm embarrassed just thinking about it."

"What?" Daniel laughed. "What kind of road trip is this?"

They talked for a bit longer and then Becky wanted to talk to her.

"Mum, I'm so stressed. I lost my anxiety ring."

Faith tried not to laugh at the irony.

When she'd finished chatting she went back into the kitchen where Anna and Niamh were cleaning up.

"Everything okay?" Anna asked.

"Oh, yes, fine. Just letting Daniel know how we were."

"Aw, that's nice. Do you guys talk every day?"

Faith thought about it.

"Yes, I suppose we do in some format or other, even when we're seeing each other, always have."

"That's so nice, especially at your age. I hope I get that," Niamh said. Faith gave her a wry smile.

People often commented on what a good marriage she and Daniel had. She supposed they did if she thought about it. But she'd only ever been with Daniel, so she had no real comparison. Sometimes she wondered if Daniel would still have married her if she hadn't ended up pregnant. Faith still felt a little guilty, and maybe a little curious what her life would have been like too if things hadn't turned out like they did.

"I don't suppose you've got *Grease* on DVD, have you, Niamh?" Anna asked.

"Mum, I don't have *anything* on DVD," Niamh said. "No one does these days."

◇

They found it on Netflix. Niamh stayed to watch the first twenty minutes and then got a series of texts that she answered furtively. Eventually she asked Anna if she would mind if she went out, and Faith and Anna watched the rest of the movie alone, before they headed out to the van to sleep for the night.

The van seemed smaller and the musty smell hadn't improved much, even with the freshly washed bedding.

"I might take a sleeping pill I think," Anna said, "I didn't sleep that well last night. Do you want one?"

"No, thanks, I'm fine," Faith said. "I sleep like the dead anyway."

They settled into their beds, talking about the movie for a while. Anna wriggled around a bit and then went quiet. Faith lay there listening to the noise of the city and thinking how great things were going. She felt like she and Anna were becoming friends, and that was nice.

Music started up further down the street but it wasn't loud or unpleasant and for a while she heard voices as people walked past, soft laughter and the metallic sound of cans. People on their way to a party maybe. Eventually, she drifted off, thinking about Sandy and her tight leather pants. The vegans would not have approved.

Chapter nine

The *Star*:

STUDENT PRANK MISTAKEN FOR ART INSTALLATION

A plumber's van was mistaken for part of an art walk today, after what the owners suspect was "just a bit of fun" from university students overnight left the pink-painted van graffitied and a large toilet concreted to its roof.

Owners Anna Sinclair and Faith Coleman were bemused to return from lunch to find a group of tourists taking photos of their Hiace.

The art-loving group had been following a SCAPE tour app and assumed the van, parked in front of a mural, was an installation piece.

Anna and Faith are heading to Invercargill in the van on Monday and say they were unsuccessful at having the lavatory removed.

"I guess it's coming with us," Anna said.

For more details on the art walk, visit scapepublicart.org.nz.

Anna groaned and half rolled out of bed. Not difficult to do when the mattress was about as wide as a plank and just as uncomfortable. For a moment she felt disorientated like she'd fallen asleep on a park bench but she thanked whatever gave her the sense to take a sleeping pill the night before because at least she'd had a decent night and hadn't even woken up to pee.

"Morning," Faith mumbled from across the van, "how did you sleep?"

"Great thanks. You?"

"Pretty good. I had a weird dream that there was an earthquake and the ground was rumbling and swaying though."

Silently they grabbed clean clothes and whatever they needed for a shower. It was still early but Niamh had assured her that she'd be up and, if not, they'd leave a key under the doormat for them. Faith stumbled out into the street first, Anna following closely behind.

"I could do with a cup of tea ..." Faith was saying and then stopped abruptly, her mouth forming a comically perfect 'o' shape. Anna followed her gaze.

Sitting on a lean in the middle of Rizzo's roof was a white, porcelain toilet. Something thick and porridgy was slapped underneath, anchoring it to the van. The 'R' from 'Rick's Plumbing' had been spray-painted over so that it now read

'Dick's Plumbing'. On both sides. There was also a crudely shaped penis on the passenger door.

"What the hell? Why would someone do that? And how? How did we not wake up?" Anna said.

"I heard a party down the road last night. Someone probably thought it would be funny. I can't believe I slept through that though."

There was a renovation happening next door to the twins' flat. A broken bathroom cabinet and several sheets of plywood leant up against the front wall. Yesterday there had probably been a discarded toilet sitting in the junk heap too.

They both stared dumbly at the van. Anna felt some surprise that it could have made itself any more conspicuous than it already was, but there you have it. She half-heartedly tried to climb up onto the roof and felt around. The cement was set dry. They headed up the steps towards the flat.

Niamh was stretched out on her yoga mat in the living room. Faith went off to have the first shower.

"Did you hear a party down the road last night? Someone seems to have cemented a toilet to the roof of our van."

"What?" Niamh got up lithely from her downward dog. "An actual loo? That's a bit random. There are always parties going on around here, so many that we don't really notice them any more. You should get Martin to have a look at it."

"Martin?" Anna asked.

"Our flatmate. He's a mechanical engineer, he's good with stuff like that. Do you want a cuppa?"

"I'd love a coffee," Anna sighed. "What have you got planned for the day?"

Martin came into the kitchen as Niamh was pouring the milk and she told him about the van vandals. He went off quite eagerly to have a look and came back shortly, grinning and clearly trying not to laugh.

"I got up and had a look but it's really well cemented down," he told them, popping four slices of bread into the toaster. "I could try to chisel it off but it'd probably break through the roof. Only thing would be to get some hydraulic shears and cut it off – but then you'd still need to replace the roof."

"We can't afford that," Anna groaned, just as Faith came in, towel wrapped around her head.

"I've sent a photo of it to a mate of mine to see if he has any ideas," Martin added.

"Rizzo," Anna explained to Faith. "Seems like we're stuck with the new renovation."

Faith looked thoughtful. "I wonder if that makes her compliant as a self-contained motorhome. A bit tricky to get to in the night though."

"And no privacy." She and Anna grinned at each other.

"You're still well under the height restriction. So unless you've got some kind of proof of who did it…" Martin's toast had popped up and he offered to put more in for them.

"… We're stuck with it. Dick's Plumbing. Always on the job," Anna said, topping up her coffee from the pot.

◇

Anna had a shower and then she and Niamh sat on her bed for a chat. Niamh told her about her classes and then mentioned she was seeing a guy casually but it wasn't serious yet.

"I'll let you know if it's meet-the-parents-worthy," she told Anna with a grin.

"Well, it might have to be separately," Anna said, watching her daughter's face.

"Yeah," Niamh said quietly. "Cameron mentioned that."

"You okay?" Anna asked.

"I dunno. I guess. It's weird to think of you guys not together, but I suppose I'll get used to it." She picked at the tassels on a cushion as she spoke. "I'm worried how Dad will cope without you. And what if he hooks up with some bimbo my age or something?"

Anna gave her a hug.

"I don't think that's going to happen, honey," she said, but she hoped for her daughter's sake she was right. Niamh had always been a daddy's girl, and Anna had suspected she would take their split the hardest.

"Things will work out," she reassured her. "Don't worry. And you know we both love you to bits."

"Yeah, and I do want you to be happy, Mum, and I know you haven't really been." She gave Anna a watery grin. "At least I'll get twice the birthday and Christmas gifts now."

Anna laughed. They hugged again, and although Anna felt emotional about telling them, she also felt hugely relieved, like a weight had lifted from her.

◇

Cameron and Martin seemed keen to go for a spin with them in Rizzo later in the morning so they all headed off for the local farmers' market with Anna driving. It was busy and she finally found a park in front of a large mural that depicted some kind of abstract Picasso-style face before she locked up and slunk away from the curious looks they were getting from passers-by. While the boys shopped for their weekly fruit and veges, Faith and Anna wandered, looking at the stalls, but Anna was conscious she didn't have a lot of cash until she'd sorted things out at the bank the next day.

Faith bought them homemade kombucha from a stall and Cameron and Martin turned up with spicy bean burritos which they ate sitting on the grass while they listened to a lone singer crooning about deadbeat lovers and broken dreams. It occurred to Anna that she didn't feel at all heartbroken about the end of her marriage. She'd been holding on for the sake of the kids for so long that it was a relief to have made that final step. Greg would just have to accept it, and if he had a hard time with that, it wasn't her problem. As well as trepidation about her future, there was also an underlying excitement. It might take a while to find where exactly she fit into this new world but she was sure that she'd figure it out eventually. Anna glanced at Faith, leaning back on her elbows sipping her drink, eyes half closed against the sun.

She gave Anna a huge smile. It seemed she already had a new friend and being here with Faith reminded her of the things she'd given up since she'd married Greg. The simple things, like eating from a food truck, shopping at an op shop, camping by a river. The expensive house and friends who only cared about what labels they wore and who they were seen with seemed so insignificant suddenly.

◇

They wandered back to the van, only to find a group of about twenty people surrounding it. They all had lanyards around their neck and most had backpacks and cameras. A man in his late twenties with a scruffy beard was standing with a notepad, talking to one of the group and taking notes.

"Umm, excuse us," she said , pushing through them to get to the driver's door.

"Wait, is this yours?" notepad guy asked.

"Yep, and we're off, so ..."

"Do you have a few minutes, just for me to ask about the creative process? Can I get your name? What was the inspiration behind the piece?"

Anna looked at his earnest face, pen poised. How odd.

"Anna Charnichael, and I imagine the inspiration was alcohol?"

"Right, right, and how long did it take?"

Faith spoke up beside her.

"It was like this when we woke up," she told him. He

looked a little lost.

"Are you one of the artists too?" he asked. The group were moving off down the road now, a woman with a clipboard herding them along. There was a lot of animated chatter and laughter.

"I'm Faith, Faith Coleman, what is this about?"

"Oaky, are you one of the artists too?"

"No, I imagine it was kids," Faith said, sounding bemused. "What is this about? Are you a reporter?

"Sorry, yes, I'm Dean Logan of the *Star*. I'm doing a piece on the SCAPE city art tour and this has been the most unexpected installation so far."

Anna started to laugh.

"Buddy, this isn't an art piece. It's some drunk students' idea of a joke."

They spent a few minutes talking to him about the van and their trip and cleared up the confusion.

"Do you mind if I included this in my piece anyway?" Dean asked.

"Go for it," Anna said.

They all got in the van, Cameron and Martin snorting with laughter in the back as they sat on the beds making jokes about how crap art was these days.

As they drove away, still chuckling, Faith said; "Well, there's something for our bucket list. Get our names in the paper."

"Yeah, but for driving around in a great big pink dunny?

Could it not have been for something a little less embarrassing?" Anna laughed.

"What a shitty day," Cameron said, making Martin snigger.

"The Pink Loo Ladies," Faith said with a grin and they spent the drive home recreating the lyrics for 'Beauty School Dropout' to things like 'Booty Loo Longdrop' and cracking themselves up.

Chapter ten

Anna dropped Faith at the supermarket in the morning to buy some supplies for the next couple of days and parked the van near the bank. She received a few sideways looks from business people as she locked Rizzo and a loud tut from an elderly man when he noticed the spray-painted penis but thankfully nobody approached her and asked her to fix their leaky sink or install a new shower head. It's not like she looked like your typical plumber this morning in her 'visit the bank manager' clothes — black skirt and heeled boots with her freshly washed angora sweater. The weather had turned cool, the air brisk, and she was glad she'd thought to pack a scarf.

The smell of coffee — real coffee, not the cheap stuff the twins drank — taunted her as she passed a cafe and her stomach growled. They hadn't eaten before they'd left that morning and she decided she'd treat herself and Faith to breakfast before they got on the road, after she'd sorted everything with the bank.

Greg had gone quiet the last couple of days and when she talked to someone with the ridiculous title of 'Relationship Manager' she found her suspicions were correct. He had indeed cut her off and removed all the money from their joint account. She still had some funds in her personal savings account and she quickly transferred the address to her parents while the bank issued her a new debit card. It wasn't ideal and she wasn't looking forward to having to deal with lawyers when she got home but for now she was going to enjoy the trip. At least she'd be able to contribute her share with Faith now.

Faith was waiting outside the bank when Anna came out, so she suggested breakfast and they headed for the little cafe Anna had passed earlier.

"I got us some wine, red and cheap, some snacks, drinks and underwear for you," Faith told her.

Anna scrunched up her nose, which made Faith laugh.

"They're fine, silly. I buy them all the time. Very comfy actually. What's the point in spending a fortune on something nobody's going to see? Triple pack for fifteen dollars."

"How can they even make them for that?" Anna was shocked. She thought of her lovely matching underwear sets. One pair of knickers cost more than three supermarket ones.

Faith inhaled the steam from her Japanese lime tea, eyes closed and a blissful expression on her face. She opened her eyes and smiled at Anna as she poured. "Don't knock 'em till you try them."

"I'll give them a go but I'll bet you I'll be hand-washing my good ones as we go."

They both ordered full breakfasts and ate with relish. The bacon was perfectly crispy. She thought briefly of Jen and Flax as she chewed.

"Do the commune ... is that the right word? Do they farm?" Anna asked.

"Yes, they farm, mostly dairy and chickens. They sell the eggs locally. My family wasn't really involved with that side of things though. My dad is a builder."

"My parents had cattle," Anna told her. "Near Otorohanga. Still do, but my older brother Mark pretty much runs it now."

"Do you see them much?"

"Not as often as I should. I used to when the kids were little. But Mark and Greg have never gotten along." She paused to finish off her coffee. "I see my younger brother a bit. He lives in Raglan. He's a surf instructor, but he has a daughter a year younger than Ben who lives with her mum in West Auckland, so he's up our way a fair bit."

"Do you surf too? "Faith asked.

"Yeah, but badly," Anna said with a grin.

"I'd love to try," Faith said. "Maybe I'll put that on my list."

"I'll get Josh to give you a lesson."

Anna ordered a second coffee and paid the bill.

"So, what about your brother?" Anna asked.

"Now that's a long story," Faith said. "I'll tell you on the way."

◇

After breakfast they wandered back to the bank car park. The wind had picked up and Anna pulled her dark scarf up around her chin to keep warm and tucked her other hand into her pocket. An armoured van was pulling into the mostly empty lot, the guards giving them an odd look as they clambered into theirs. Anna put the key into the ignition. It took several tries to get the engine to turn over, which was a bit of a worry. She gave the accelerator a good rev to make sure it kept running and looked in her mirrors to back out. There was a massive *BANG* and then the guards were shouting. She could see them in the rear-view mirror lying on the ground, arms over their heads. One of them was shouting into his walkie-talkie and the doors to the bank were suddenly closing, large metal grilles sliding down. An alarm sounded, its piercing pulse sounding like it was in the van with them.

"What the heck is going on?" Faith said nervously, pulling off her black beanie and opening the door to look out.

"Stay where you are!" a guard shouted. "The police are on the way and we have no access to the back of our vehicle."

"What on the earth?" Anna said. Was the bank being robbed? She wound down her window and called out, "What's going on? Are we in danger?"

A guard called back: "Are you willing to surrender your

weapon?" She and Faith shared a confused look. Weapon? They thought she might have a gun? Did they think they could borrow it?

"Us? Why on the earth would we have a gun?" One of the security guards looked up from where he lay on the asphalt. He gave his partner an exasperated look. Then he called back to Anna.

"Did you just fire a weapon, miss?" Anna thought it was nice he'd said miss, not Mrs, and gave him a warm smile. Then remembered he was waiting for an answer.

"Ahh, no. I didn't. I've never even held one. Even though my dad always wanted me to go hunting with him ..." she trailed off as the guard got to his feet, giving his partner a disgusted look as he brushed down his pants and then started speaking into his walkie-talkie again. The other guard, blushing furiously, went over to the bank entrance.

"Sorry, looks like we overreacted," the guard continued. He was very cute, Anna noted. "I think maybe it was just your engine backfiring."

Anna started to laugh. The idea of her and Faith as bank robbers was hilarious.

"Did you really think we'd rob a bank and use this as a getaway car?" she said. "It's hardly inconspicuous, is it?"

He looked rather mortified.

"It's Ritchie's first week," he muttered as if to explain things. "Sorry for the misunderstanding."

Anna and Faith laughed all the way out of Christchurch.

Chapter eleven

New Zealand Herald:

HILARY BARRY IN DEEP DO-DO FOR TOILET HUMOUR

Seven Sharp presenter Hilary Barry is once again under fire for what some viewers saw as inappropriate language. The iconic NZ celeb was most amused after an incident at a Christchurch bank where a hot-pink plumbing van with its own rooftop dunny was involved in a mistaken attempt at a bank robbery.

While detailing the debacle, Hilary commented that the two getaway drivers would have been in "deep @*%!" if caught.

Several complaints were made to the Broadcasting Commission. When asked for a comment, Hilary replied: "It's a nice change from disgust at my cleavage."

Meanwhile, the 'Dick's Plumbing' van is going viral on Snapchat and Instagram as students try to get photos of the very visible vehicle.

Faith was still grinning an hour later as they drove through Ashburton.

"So, tell me about your brother then," Anna said, tooting at a group of kids pointing at them from the school playground.

"Oh, right, Isaac. Yeah." Faith paused to gather her thoughts. "So you have to take into account I was only eight when he left. I didn't really understand the drama. It wasn't really until I was in high school that I started to realise why he'd gone. My only friend outside the commune kind of pieced it together for me. And then one of my older sisters filled me in on the details much later."

Anna gave her a questioning look, and she rummaged in the supermarket bag for a bit to open a bag of lollies first.

"Isaac is gay," she said, "and in my parents' eyes, that is the ultimate sin. Worse than premarital sex, worse than adultery, worse than anything."

"Oh shit. And your parents found out?"

"Yeah, I think so, and then they started talking about suitable matches for a marriage. He told them he wouldn't do it. They tried to do I guess what was their own version of conversion therapy with him and the elders but it didn't work, of course. He left when he was eighteen. The day he turned eighteen actually."

"Oh man, poor guy," Anna said. "So when did you see him

again?"

"Well, I didn't. And he turns fifty next week, so it's been a long time." Faith felt a bit teary at the thought. She was also a bit nervous.

"Wow. So, how did you get back in touch?"

"Daniel encouraged me to actually. Charity and I stayed in touch a bit once I left and she stayed in touch with Isaac. But we never talked about him at all. It was a forbidden subject and it just became a habit, you know?" Anna nodded. "Anyway, Daniel said I should just ask, and when I did, I found out she knew where he was, and I reached out."

"Aww, and was he happy you did?"

"Yeah, so happy. He moved to Invercargill and got a job and then he met his partner Keith when he was twenty-one. They've been together ever since.

"And you never saw each other?"

"Oh, we FaceTime. So it won't be a major shock to see each other after all these years. He doesn't know I'm coming though. It's a surprise."

"Oh wow, how cool. Is Charity going too?"

Faith frowned. She always felt so sad when she thought of Charity.

"No, she's still in the community with the others. I never lost contact with her but we can't talk often. Early on I tried to persuade her to leave but she wouldn't."

"How come?"

"I don't really know. I guess she still believes? She married

Jebediah when she was sixteen but they never had any kids. She says she's barren, but it could have been him, you know? And she's so ... I don't even know... guilty about it? ... that I think she feels obligated to stay. I don't know for sure but it seems like she and Jebediah don't hate each other either, which is saying something."

"Oh man, that is sad."

"Yeah, but she's close to my nieces and nephews, and in the commune kids are sort of all treated like your own, even if they're not, sort of 'village to raise a family'. It's one of the things I did like about that place."

"Yeah, there's definitely something to be said for that," Anna agreed, reaching for another lolly.

"So what does Isaac do?"

"He's a signwriter. He was lucky enough to get taken on straight from school and now he owns his own company."

"And what about his man?"

"Keith's retired actually. He's quite a bit older than Isaac. But he used to be in banking." Faith grinned. "You'll love this. He's a major royalist. Like obsessed with the royal family. He and Isaac have spent the last five or so years building a replica house of Buckingham Palace. They're opening up to the public as a sort of museum."

"Oh, my God, that's hilarious," Anna said "But who's the Queen?"

Faith laughed. "It gets better. They have corgis too. And they've all been named after different royals. I think at the moment they have three. Andrew, Harry and Charlotte."

"What a crack-up. I bet you'll have an amazing time."

"You should come with me."

"Oh really? I wouldn't want to impose."

Faith was about to reply when there was a thump and then the car started to shake and then slide sideways. Anna braked and managed to pull the van over to the side of the road as it made a loud flapping noise. Thankfully there was very little traffic.

"Golly, what was that?" Faith asked.

"Flat tyre, I think."

They got out and Faith went round to Anna's side. Sure enough, the back tyre was looking very deflated and on closer inspection, Anna found a large nail embedded in it.

"What do we do now?" Faith asked, feeling a bit useless. Daniel always dealt with any car stuff, since she had been almost thirty when she finally got her licence.

"Hope like hell this thing has a good spare and a jack," said Anna. "And that I can remember how to change a tyre. I haven't had to for years."

They finally found the jack in the compartment of the sliding door, and then Anna started to wriggle her way under the van holding the wrench to remove the spare.

Faith was busting for a wee, so she told Anna she would be right back, and went to the side of the road looking for somewhere to go. It was all flat plains, but there was no traffic in sight, so she decided to just do a quick squat.

Just as she was finishing, there was a loud toot and a station wagon went past, a load of teenagers hanging out the window with their phones aimed at the van, yelling and cheering. Mortified, she pulled up her pants and went back to tell Anna, only to find her sticking half out the van, her skirt ruched up and her fancy red satin knickers on full display as she wriggled back out.

"What were they saying?" Anna asked.

"Something about there being no dicks in sight," Faith told her.

Chapter twelve

New Zealand Herald:

POLICE APPEAL TO PUBLIC FOR HELP LOCATING HISTORIC HAND

Police have had no luck finding Captain Cook's stolen and preserved hand, which was removed from an exhibition at Te Papa last week, despite extensive investigations.

Police commissioner Aaron Coster says every effort is going into finding the priceless artifact, but that so far, their leads have not turned up the results they would have liked.

"Please, if you took this irreplaceable piece of history, or know who did, I urge you to contact authorities," Mr Coster said in a statement this morning. He says they have not ruled out offering a reward for the hand's return, but says as of today, the search for the culprit is still ongoing.

They drove for another hour. The landscape was dull and dry and there wasn't much to see of interest. It was all brown/green farmland and road works. Large logging trucks and milk tankers overtook them constantly, their tyres churning up dust and heat as they rattled past. Time seemed to pause as they drove past what felt like the same landmarks over and over. The plan was to drive straight to Oamaru, but when they got to Timaru and spotted a sign for a penguin colony at Caroline Bay, Anna suggested it was time for a break. They were well behind schedule with all the bank drama and the flat tyre, but she needed to stretch her legs, wash her greasy hands and get a caffeine fix.

They pulled up outside a small cafe right on the beach, drawing the attention of the locals, many of whom took out their phones to take a picture of the van. They both needed the loo, so they detoured to the bathroom first, before getting a table on the wooden deck, the briny smell of the ocean mixing with the smell of roasting coffee.

Outside, the beach was mostly empty, the wind whipping sand up in whorls against the rocks. A lone figure walked slowly along the foreshore, bending occasionally to pick something up and put it into a basket. Their red sweatshirt stood out starkly against the colourless sky.

A smiling blonde waitress with long false nails sidled up with menus and took their drinks order. When she came back she gave them another big smile, pink lipstick smudged on her front tooth.

"Youse guys are in the van right?" she asked, setting Anna's coffee down in front of Faith, slopping it slightly onto the saucer.

"We are," Anna said, switching the drinks over.

"That's so cool. I saw your page. I'm stoked. I'll get to post on it now. You're probably the most famous people we've had in here since that time the *Wilderpeople* kid came in."

Faith was grinning away behind her menu. Anna could tell by her eyes. She wasn't sure what to say so she thanked the girl, who told them her name was Chloe, and gave her her lunch order.

"Do you think she read the art walk article?" Faith said.

"Maybe. What page was she talking about though?"

Chloe returned with their salads and waved out the window at the person in red, who was coming up the beach.

"That's Red," she told them. "He's an artist. Like sculpting and stuff." She pointed to a piece on the wall to Anna's right. It was a driftwood piece that looked like a morepork in flight. It was rather beautiful.

"Oh wow, that's amazing," Faith said, standing to take a closer look.

"Does he live locally?" Anna asked Chloe.

"I don't think he lives anywhere," she said. "He just turns up sometimes, either to collect wood, or sell his work to cafes. He's a free spirit." She sounded rather wistful. "No one knows his real name, so we all call him Red, 'cause of his top. He doesn't speak much."

Faith returned to the table.

"Well, he's underselling himself. That piece is amazing and it's at least half the price it should be."

"There's a few more by the counter," Chloe told her.

They ate in silence for a bit, watching the water and talking about the penguins. It had started to drizzle and Anna was feeling less inclined to brave the elements, especially since all she had were her heeled boots.

"I don't suppose you have a spare jacket?" she asked Faith.

"No, and the rain looks like it's settling in a bit now too. Perhaps we should flag the beach? It's getting a bit late too."

Anna looked along the beach, but there was no sign of Red. She wondered where he went when it rained.

"You know, I might get one of those driftwood pieces for Isaac," Faith said. "I bet he'd love it."

They went over to the counter to pay and then looked at the other pieces. There was a whale, a fish and, amazingly, a dog. It wasn't a corgi, but Faith was thrilled and after Chloe had wrapped it in tissue and brown string, they headed back to the van, making a quick dash to avoid the rain that was now coming down quite heavily.

Anna had gotten another coffee to go which she settled into the centre console before starting the van. It lurched into life with another backfire and they pulled out of the car park laughing.

"I hope we don't get another puncture," Anna said as they got back onto the main road. "We need to get the flat repaired in Dunedin, I guess."

They'd been driving for about ten minutes when a figure walking on the side of the road caught their attention, red sweatshirt drenched, and his thumb out.

"Oh, it's Red." Anna looked questioningly at Faith, who nodded, and they pulled over a few metres in front of him, the van lurching in a pothole. A large milk tanker thundered past, kicking muddy water against the side of the van.

Red walked up to Faith's window and she wound it down a notch.

"Jump in," she told him, indicating the sliding side door.

He did, placing his basket and a backpack in the centre and hunched over, looking at the beds, before pulling off his sodden sweatshirt. His T-shirt rose with it and Anna felt like she and Faith were recreating *Thelma & Louise* for a minute as Red's toned stomach came into view. A dragon tattoo swirled down into his jeans, the colours shimmering against his olive skin. When his head emerged, she gulped. He was beautiful. Long dark hair, full lips, gorgeous green eyes. But he was also not much older than Cameron, she guessed, and took her mind out of the gutter and gave him a nice, mum-like smile.

"Hi, Red. I'm Anna, this is Faith."

"Thanks for stopping," he said, perching on Anna's bed with a wince.

"No problem. There's an old towel in that crate," she told him. "So, where are you headed? We're going to Dunedin."

She looked at her watch. "Or at least Oamaru."

"Waimate," he said. He was shivering with cold and when he reached into his bag, only drew out a thin top to pull on. Anna took her coffee and offered it to him. He took it with a grateful smile, rubbing at his hair with the towel and then sipping at it, hands cupped around it for warmth.

Anna turned up the heater and then pulled back out onto the highway.

"Where's Waimate?" Faith asked.

"Just past Hook," he told her. "There's fine."

Faith was googling on her phone. "Oh, I think we can drop you there. It's only another ten minutes." She looked over at Anna who agreed.

"I just got one of your art pieces," Faith said. "You're very talented."

"Oh, thanks." Anna could see him in the rear-view mirror and he was blushing. God, he was adorable.

"So, what's in Waimate?" she asked.

"My grandmother," he told her, but didn't elaborate.

Faith rustled in her shopping bag and produced some beef jerky, offering it to him. He gave her a smile and accepted it and they drove with just the sound of the van's windscreen wipers scraping against the glass, and the odd weird little rattle of the engine to break the rhythm. Every now and then the weird rattle became a kind of thumping noise. Anna wasn't familiar with ancient Hiace vans and hoped it was something to do with Rizzo's elderly status – perhaps vehicular arthritis.

"Not great weather for hitching," Faith said, swivelling in her seat to look at Red. Anna wondered whether she found him as attractive as she did. When Faith bent towards her and whispered 'Thelma and Louise', she guessed she did. She raised her eyebrows at Faith.

"What? It's not like I've never seen any movies. Daniel and I had a DVD player. And I mean – Brad Pitt." She turned her attention back to Red.

"Been in worse," he said. Rizzo thumped loudly in reply. "That doesn't sound good," he said.

Anna gripped the wheel, peering through the windscreen. They'd reached Hook and soon came to the turnoff leading to Waimate. It was still pelting down and she indicated to turn.

"Here's good."

Faith didn't think there would be much chance of him getting another ride.

"Don't be silly, it's fine, it's not far. Besides, we might look at stopping for the night."

"You could park up in Gran's driveway if you want. She likes company. Says I don't talk enough." As if he'd already said more than usual, he fell silent.

"Well, the temperature gauge has gone up, might be an idea to give Rizzo a rest."

"Maybe I could have a go at driving tomorrow," Faith said. "I feel bad that I'm just sitting here eating the snacks." She held out the packet of Fruit Bursts to Anna, who took an orange one, and then offered them to Red.

"You don't have to, I really don't mind," Anna said.

"No, I'd quite like to actually. It would get me over this weird thing that I have where the only time I've ever driven a manual was when I was learning to drive. I skidded off the road and into a fence. Maybe it would reverse the bad juju."

Anna hoped it would seem she was concentrating on driving rather than that she looked nervous at this declaration.

"Daniel bought me a little Toyota Corolla after that. Automatic. I still have it now."

A far call from Anna's new car every two years. And for what? Did it make her any happier? she wondered as she glanced over at Faith whose mouth was quirked into a smile. The fence incident can't have been too traumatic. Hopefully she wasn't that bad of a driver.

◇

They drove straight through the township. From what Anna could see, it had that pleasant but slightly neglected feel small towns often have. The kind of place you usually wanted to leave as soon as you could if you'd grown up there but then yearned to return to once you were old and jaded. There was a cafe, she noted, closed now but it could be good the next morning for coffee before they got on the road, and a Caltex service station as they should probably fill up on petrol.

Red directed her to turn off the road and his grandmother's property was a short drive into the countryside, nestled between farmland on one side and a heavily wooded area on two others. It was a squat, white brick house, smoke billowing from a chimney in a welcoming way with heavy lace curtains in the windows. There was a two-bay garage, in front of which was a large asphalted parking area, just as Red had promised. Anna parked as close to the house as she could and they got out slamming the doors and running through the rain to the front porch.

Red pushed open the door and Anna and Faith followed him inside. The heavy, rich smell of roasting lamb and wood-smoke greeted them and Anna's stomach rumbled. It was cosy and warm after the dank cold outside.

"Hello, sweet, oh, you've brought visitors." A woman appeared in the hallway, large bosomed with curly grey hair, wiping her hands on the tea towel slung over her shoulder. She held out her hands to Red, grasping his in her own. "What cold hands you have. Come and get warm in front of the fire." She looked questioningly at Red and then at the two strangers who had appeared unannounced in her house, but didn't seem overly fazed.

"This is Anna and Faith," Red mumbled. "They're headed to Dunners. I said it would be okay if they parked their camper outside overnight."

The woman smiled warmly at them and held out a hand. "Joyce," she told them. "Of course you're welcome to stay. I hope you'll have some dinner with us. I've a huge roast on and I was just about to put some veggies in so it's no trouble to throw in a few extras."

"We don't want to be a bother," Faith said weakly. Anna's stomach gave another loud growl.

"You brought my young man all the way out here and saved him from the weather, so you're no bother. Besides, he's not much of a one for conversation. Do either of you play Scrabble?"

"Can we help you to do anything?" Faith asked, but Joyce shook her head. "Come and warm up. Can I get you a sherry? Glass of wine maybe?"

"Oh, thank you. We actually have wine in the van. I'll get it," Anna said as Faith removed her shoes and followed Joyce down the hall.

"I'll go," Red volunteered and she handed him the keys with a smile.

"In the supermarket bag in the passenger seat, thanks."

The living room was crowded with well-worn furniture, and a cosy wood-burner glowed invitingly. There was an eclectic collection of pictures on the walls, from landscape watercolours to Red's modern artwork, family portraits — including a large framed photo of a man in his thirties with his arm around a much younger looking Red.

"My son," Joyce said, noticing Anna looking. "He worked at the sawmill before he got laid off. He's got a woodcutting business near Methven now."

"Are you sure we're not imposing?" Faith asked.

"No, not at all," Joyce insisted, taking out several wine glasses from a small corner unit. Red returned, wine in hand and even more soaked. "Why don't you have a hot shower," Joyce told him. "And throw your clothes in the machine. You're leaving a big puddle."

He handed the wine over and gave her a kiss on the cheek before heading back down the hall. Joyce sighed as she poured the wine.

"I'm so relieved he's back," she told Anna as she passed out the drinks. "I worry so much when I know he's out in this sort of weather. You really are lovely to pick him up and bring him home."

"Oh, it's no trouble, really," Anna said. "Does he live with you then?"

"On and off," Joyce told her with a sad smile. "He's a bit of a gypsy that boy, but he knows I like his company. It can get lonely out here on my own. Although I do have Grey."

"Is that your son?" Faith asked.

"Oh no, dear, that's my ..." A low growl came from the kitchen then and the sound of claws on the lino before a huge snout and raised ears appeared in the doorway. Faith made a little squeaking noise and took a few steps back before sinking onto the couch. What appeared to be a large silver wolf padded into the lounge and pressed its nose into Joyce's hand.

"... dog," Joyce finished. She looked over at Faith and

chuckled. "He's harmless, honestly, a real softy."

He was a husky, Anna thought, or perhaps a mix with Alsatian. She bent down and held out a fist for him to sniff. He came over instantly and then sat, paw raised to shake her hand. He was gorgeous. She gave him a good pat and rubbed his ears, which he loved, until Red returned and she was abandoned so Grey could go crazy for the young man.

"Grey adores him," Joyce said fondly. "Dogs are very good at judging character, I believe." Anna agreed. She had always wanted a dog but Greg hated them. She suspected he was actually afraid of them but wouldn't admit it. She imagined Grey would hate Greg. It made her grin.

"Gran, where's the hairdryer gone?" he asked, rubbing at his hair with a towel and trying to keep it from Grey.

"Oh, it broke, sorry, love. I had to throw it out. The motor burnt out, left a scorch mark on the counter too."

"When was this?"

"Oh, a week or so ago. I'll get a new one soon, but it's down the list a bit, I'm afraid. The pension doesn't really allow for luxuries like hairdryers."

"I'll keep an eye out in the thrift stores," he told her and she gave him a beaming smile before turning to Anna and Faith.

"Right, so tell me all about yourselves," she said, sitting in a brocade armchair. "What brings you to Waimate?"

"Well, it's a funny story really," Anna said. "It started as a bad drunken idea but it's turned out to be a lovely adventure."

"Well, now I'm intrigued," Joyce said, leaning forward in her chair.

They told her about the van, and their decision to take a road trip. Anna didn't mention her marriage, just that she'd gone to see her kids and that they were heading to Invercargill. Faith filled her in on Isaac and the palace.

"Well, now that sounds like something I'd go to see," Joyce said. "I saw Charles and Diana back in '83 when they were newly married. That woman was in a class of her own." Her face softened at the memory, then hardened. "I didn't bother when he came with that awful Camilla. Home-wrecking hussy." They both tried not to laugh.

"Has your brother always been a royalist then?" she asked Faith, who shook her head.

"No, I doubt he'd even heard of the royal family as a child," she said. Joyce gave her a questioning look. "We grew up in the Servants of Christ," she said, and Joyce's eyes went wide, her hand rising to her chest like she'd had disturbing news. Anna covered her laugh.

"Oh, my goodness," Joyce said. "Well, that's a big can of worms."

◇

After finishing off the wine, and having a lovely roast dinner, they sat and talked while Red offered to take the dog for a quick walk.

"Take your granddad's coat in the hall cupboard," Joyce

told him. "It's not like he's using it," she said sadly. He gave her another kiss on the cheek and slunk out.

"Sad," Joyce told them. "His father and my late husband had a falling out when he was about the same age. We've only seen each other a handful of times since. I lost so much of their lives. And all over something silly. He hates me now, despite all my efforts to fix things."

"Oh, I'm sorry to hear that," Anna said. The fire was on, the house warm and inviting and Joyce seemed so lovely. She couldn't imagine anyone hating her.

"I'm sure he doesn't hate you," Faith said, reaching over and patting Joyce's hand. "I haven't seen my parents for a long, long time and things aren't great, but I don't hate them."

"Well, darling, all I can say is, if you can make amends, do it. You never know when it'll be too late. And there's nothing worse than things staying unresolved." She took a hanky from her pocket and dabbed at her eyes.

"Well, that's enough doom and gloom from me," she said with a little laugh. Anna smiled and looked over at Faith. Her face was contemplative.

"Well, I think perhaps it's time we turn in," she said. "Thank you so much though for dinner."

"My pleasure, love," Joyce said. "Will you be warm enough out there?"

"We'll be fine."

They used the bathroom and headed back out to the van,

the air crisp after the warmth of the house, but the rain now just an unrushed plinking on the roof as they got settled into their beds.

"Poor Joyce," said Anna, "that must be hard not having your child around. She's lucky she's got Red." Faith murmured in agreement. A thought occurred to her. "I wonder what his real name is."

But Faith was already asleep.

Chapter thirteen

Waimate Advertiser:

PORTA-POTTY PASSES THROUGH

A distinctive pink plumber's van has become something of a media sensation after an Instagram page was set up to track its movements across the country. After Christchurch students allegedly attached a toilet to the roof, it has become a badge of honour to get a snapshot of the vehicle as it heads south.

Caroline Bay Cafe worker Chloe Turner managed to snap a shot of the van and post it to the page.

"It's more exciting than the time that movie kid was here," she told our reporter. The van was last seen on the main road south.

Faith slid open the door the next morning and found herself staring at a kangaroo. She'd spent a large part of the night having weird dreams involving her parents and she paused for a bit to contemplate whether she was actually still asleep. The small furry creature looked up at her, seemingly less fazed by her appearance than she was by it. It regarded her solemnly for a beat, ear flicking, and then calmly continued chewing.

The sound of a door opening had it looking up, and then it was off, hopping across the lawn, tail out behind it. Grey came down the path, giving a half-hearted bark, before meandering over to a bush to pee. Red appeared, back in his hoodie, basket in hand. "Hey."

"Morning. Am I going mad or was that a kangaroo?"

"Wallaby," he said with a shrug.

Anna sat up, her hair a tangled mess, rubbing at her face. "What? What did I miss?"

"There was a wallaby here. On the lawn," Faith told her.

"What? We don't have wallabies in New Zealand, do we?" She looked far less poised than usual. Less put together and far less intimidating. More human.

"Yeah, there's heaps out here. Pests," Red told her, whistling for Grey and setting off across the lawn to a chicken coop.

"Wow. Well, that's not something you see every day," Faith said, getting out and stretching. "How cool. I wish I'd got a photo."

Joyce was up and making porridge when they knocked on the door. They took turns having a quick shower. When

Faith went in after Anna she noticed the scorch mark on the sink bench and then a fancy-looking hairdryer plugged into the socket beside it. They joined Joyce at the Formica table which was set, lace doily over the sugar pot and a knitted cosy over the teapot.

"You're famous," she told them with a laugh, laying the paper down in front of them.

"I'm glad I didn't see that van of yours last night – I'd have thought you were both barmy."

On the page was a photo from the cafe. The van even in black and white stood out glaringly against the backdrop of the beach. The toilet perched on the top had a seagull standing on the seat. Thankfully, neither of them was in the picture.

◇

They set off after breakfast, leaving a twenty-dollar note under the teapot to say thank you.

Joyce gave them both a hug and then put something in Faith's hand. It was a soft-pink crystal. "Rose quartz," she told her. "Good for healing rifts."

Faith gave her an awkward smile and put it into her pocket, then climbed into the van.

"Oh, I almost forgot," she said to Anna. "You forgot your hairdryer in the bathroom."

Anna looked weirdly embarrassed.

"I didn't forget it," she said quietly. "I just figured I didn't really need it that badly."

Faith looked at her new friend, looking awkward at getting caught out doing something nice. She might appear to be a bit of a high-maintenance, high-society woman, but she was a lot more faceted than that, Faith realised. Instead of embarrassing her further, she started the van acting unaffected.

"Yeah, not much use for one in this old girl," she said and they were off down the road in a reluctant Rizzo, who was rattling somewhat ominously, hoping to see another wallaby as they drove out of town and back onto the main road.

By the time they were ten minutes in, Faith realised she'd overthought the whole manual car thing. Rizzo was quite easy to drive really and she should have done it sooner.

"Right, so tell me more about the commune," Anna said. "I'm dying to know all the juicy details."

Faith laughed. "Like what?"

"What did you wear? Do they have arranged marriages? Do you go to hospitals? I don't know, it's all just a bit fascinating."

"Well, yes, the elders choose your spouse. Hospitals are a bit of a grey area. We could go for broken legs, some surgeries and things – we're not anti blood products or anything like that – but stuff like cancer? That's seen as God's will, so ..."

They spent the next half hour talking about Faith's upbringing. She was used to people's curiosity. After years living a normal life she could see how odd the lifestyle was.

She'd grown up with very set gender roles. The women cooked and cleaned and did laundry; clothes were demure and plain. They were to be submissive to the men, and worked only as teachers, midwives or nurses and occasionally as office workers. And only within the commune and until they had children, which they birthed at home.

"It's funny, I acclimated well when I left, I think, but I had a lot of weird guilt after the girls were born when I went on the pill. It seemed such a big thing, to stop nature, God's will."

"So you still believe in God?"

"Well, I believe in something. Maybe not the same God as my parents and sisters, but something ... higher."

"So had they chosen someone for you to marry?" Anna asked.

"Yep, Josiah Burns. Nice enough guy but I wasn't at all keen on him."

"Haha, you'd have been Faith Burns," Anna said with a laugh. "I can't imagine who my parents might have picked for me given the chance. Probably Terry Grogan. Ergh." She looked over at Faith and grinned. "Nose-picker." Faith laughed. The van made a loud beeping noise.

"Shit, there's an orange light that's come on on the dash," Faith said. "What's it for?"

"No idea. Hopefully nothing important."

"Should we stop?"

"I don't think there's much point. I can change a tyre and check the oil, but that's about all my car expertise. If we open the hood I have no idea what I'm looking at."

"Well, that's more than me," Faith confessed.

"I'm sure it'll be fine. Let's get to Dunedin and we can look at it then," Anna said. She seemed confident, opening up a bag of M&M's, and they went back to talking about the Servants of Christ.

"So were you allowed to watch TV?"

"Nope."

"What about books?"

"Some, but mostly non-fiction stuff."

"What about magazines?"

"No, definitely not."

"So what did you do for porn?" Anna asked, making Faith crack up.

◇

They stopped in Dunedin for lunch and parked in a large parking lot. The van made a pained grinding noise as they pulled in and Faith realised a little belatedly that she'd forgotten to change down gears.

They used the bathrooms and had lunch at a Mediterranean cafe, sitting in an enclosed courtyard with olive and lemon trees in large tubs.

"I might get a coffee to go," Anna said as she scraped up the last of the hummus from their mezze platter. "Hey, who's that out by the van?"

Faith looked at where she was pointing. A scruffy-looking guy in faded baggy jeans and a puffer vest was lurking around the van's side door, looking furtive.

"I'll go check," Faith told her. "You get your coffee."

She wandered out to the parking lot, where the guy was now tugging on the sliding door.

"Can I help you?" she asked, and he spun around, hands going into his pockets.

"Oh, hey, umm, I just locked myself out, it's all good," he told her. He was only in his twenties, she would say. His hair was buzzed short, with a few scars visible on his scalp and one eyebrow. There was a slightly vacant look about his eyes and she wondered if he was high.

"Okay, well, I think you've got the wrong van, mate, this one's mine." She held out the keys to show him. His mouth dropped open and he frowned.

"Oh, yeah, but like I mean ... It was my mate's van. Baz. 'Cept it didn't have the loo on it." He chewed on his bottom lip. "I'm Gary. His mate."

"Oh right, Baz. Yeah, he sold it to us in Wellington," Faith told him, "at a party."

The kid shuffled around kicking at the kerb with his off-white sneaker.

"Yeah, but like I had something in there, and I need it back." He looked up at her and gave her a lopsided smile. "Can I just get it? It won't take long."

Faith wondered what he could have left in the van that they hadn't found. Then she realised.

"Oh, right, hang on," she told him, unlocking the passenger door and leaning into the glove box. "Here you go." She passed him the rap CD with a smile. "Not really our kind of music anyway."

The guy gave her a funny look and opened his mouth to speak just as a large group of students appeared all yelling and cheering and pulling out their phones.

"Dude, it's legit the van," someone yelled.

Anna appeared carrying a takeaway cup and gave her an eye-roll. "Let's go, shall we?"

Faith went round to the driver's door and hopped in, hoping she didn't embarrass herself as she put it into reverse and backed the van out. Baz's friend was getting into a small red car parked beside them and she gave him a quick wave as she changed into first and left.

"Who was that?" Anna asked.

"A friend of the mysterious Baz," Faith told her. "He said he left something in here and needed it back."

"Oh, the drugs?"

"Oh, my goodness, I didn't even think of that. I thought he meant the CD. No wonder he looked confused."

"Well, if he knew Baz from Wellington, it's a long way to go for a shitty rap CD," Anna said with a laugh.

◇

They stopped for gas on the way out of town and Anna noticed there was a tyre shop next door so they pulled up outside, Rizzo spluttering loudly. There was a beefy man in a checked shirt in the workshop and he came out to meet them, wiping his hands on a dirty rag.

"Hey there, ladies, you need a bit of help?"

"We're just after a tyre repair," Anna said. "We got a flat a little while ago — I think maybe a nail might have gone through it."

"Oh, you do, do you?"

"I'm pretty sure," Anna said.

"Well, how about you let me be the judge of that? I'll fix you up with a nice new tyre and then you can go on your way to the shops, or whatever it is you ladies do. We'll have the van back to hubby in no time."

"What makes you think it's not our van?" Anna's cheeks were flushed red with indignation.

"What? You telling me you two are actually plumbers? Well, if you can fix my broken loo, I'll give you your tyre for free, how's that?" He chuckled and shook his head in amusement.

"Okay, done," Anna told him. She jerked open the van door and indicated the flat tyre to Beefcheeks. He gave them an appraising look and then as if to call their bluff, he pointed to a shipping container that had been fitted out as an office.

"Through there, door on the left."

"Anna," Faith hissed as he stalked off. "What are you doing?"

"I don't know, he just pissed me off, assuming just because we're women that we wouldn't know how to fix a loo."

"Yeah, but we don't actually know, do we?"

"How hard can it be? We've got tools." She grabbed them from the back of the van and waved her phone. "And YouTube."

◇

"I think it's the fill valve," Faith said, looking up from Anna's phone five minutes later. They had an assortment of wrenches laid across the filthy bathroom floor. She shuffled through the tool box. "I don't think there's anything here to replace it though."

"It might just be a washer," Anna said doubtfully, peering over Faith's shoulder. "This bit here looks a bit worn out. It's kind of like a bottle top. What if we just pulled it off and put a water bottle lid on in its place, and stuck a new washer on? That could work."

"It's worth a try, I guess. How much would it cost to call out a real plumber? We're probably saving him a heap."

Anna snuck back out to the van and unscrewed the top of her water bottle. Beefcheeks was nowhere in sight but she could hear a hissing noise coming from within the workshop. She hurried back inside, taking a bracing deep breath before stepping back into the urine-soaked bathroom.

"Try this."

Faith banged the valve with a wrench to dislodge the broken part and they slid the bottle top on. They used a handful of washers to hold everything in place and Anna replaced everything inside and wedged the lid down. They put their tools back into the box and thoroughly washed their hands with lukewarm water and a cracked and dirty cake of soap before retreating into the waiting room.

Beefcheeks came in about ten minutes later. "Well, just as I thought, you must've run over a nail. Tyres still pretty good so I did a repair. No need for a new one."

As they stood to leave, Faith nudged Anna. Her eyes were wide in horror and she indicated with her head towards the bathroom. A thin trickle of water had started to seep out under the door.

"No need for paperwork," Faith said hurriedly, hefting the tool box into her right hand. "I wouldn't use the toilet for a little while though, it needs to, er, settle first."

"We should have stuffed some loo paper down it," Anna hissed as they hurried to the van. "Do you think we were meant to turn off the water?"

Anna buckled her seatbelt as Faith started the engine. "Oh shoot," she exclaimed, glancing into the rear-vision mirror. Anna craned her head to see what Faith was looking at. Beefcheeks was running out of the office, waving one meaty fist at them. With a sudden roar, Faith gunned the engine and swung onto the road, tyres squealing. When Anna looked over at her she was grinning broadly. "Thelma and Louise!" she yelled, looking slightly wild.

◇

The van was still making a clunking sound, but they'd sort of gotten used to its rhythmic tempo now. They headed out of town, feeling a little guilty at their shoddy plumbing job and thinking they had probably done nothing to change the tyre guy's sexist views on women plumbers.

"He did say he was going to give us a tyre though," Faith pointed out. "All he did was put a crappy patch on it in the end. I reckon fair's fair."

They both grinned at each other as they picked up speed down the long straight highway.

◇

"So why social work?" Anna asked Faith a little while later.

"Well, I never really wanted to be a nurse," she told Anna. "That was just a way out of the whole arranged marriage. And something my father was sort of on board with, with the idea I could do midwifery, I suspect. But once I was out there, and Daniel and I got settled into life, I realised my life experience might actually help someone, you know? And I love my job, especially when I work with teens."

"Good on you. Really. Your story is so fascinating. Makes me feel very dull and boring."

Faith had never really thought of herself as interesting. It gave her pause. Perhaps there were just different ways of living life, and hers hadn't been as wasted as she sometimes thought.

"So tell me about the chef thing then,' she said. "What's your favourite thing to cook?"

"Oh, baking for sure. I used to love doing fancy dinners

and things, but I've done so many work dinners it's old. No, baking. I love the exactness of it. The science. And the art, the decorating and presenting ..."

Anna looked so animated, and Faith opened her mouth to say so when the van suddenly made an awful grinding noise, like metal on metal.

"Flippin' heck," Faith said as it lurched, stalled and then shuddered slowly to a stop. She steered it off to the side of the road, wobbling over the uneven ground and coming to a final rest on a lean at the verge, facing a drain. The engine clunked and whirred and then popped with an ominous hiss, like a last gasping breath before it died entirely.

Chapter fourteen

Bode Chronicle:

COMMUNITY 'COPS A LOOK' FOR CHARITY

Locals turned out in droves last Saturday to support Bode Playcentre's latest fundraising effort. Hoping to install shade sails for their outdoor play area, the team set up a charity auction that raised over $600 for the centre.

The highlight of the evening had to be the final 'Win a Date' auction, with our favourite police officer Kurt Baker getting his kit off to entice the ladies. The lucky recipient, Donna Jameson, declared it was the best $150 she'd spent in a long time. Her husband, Brett, joked that he should have put in a higher bid on the six-month membership to Fitz Gym.

Local cafe owner Mary Duncan was also thrilled with her loot in the mystery box auction, which set her back $80, but remained tight-lipped about who she would be taking with her for the romantic horse and cart ride for two.

"Shit," Anna said, banging her hand down on the dashboard, causing the glove box to fly open. At least something in this shit-heap worked, she thought without much humour.

"I'm sorry, I'm never driving a manual again," Faith moaned. "I knew I had bad karma. Maybe it's payback for being fake plumbers."

"Don't be silly, she's been making protesting noises at us for ages and we ignored it. We should have got someone to take a look in Dunedin."

Wearily they got out of Rizzo. Faith eventually found the lever to pop the bonnet and they stood peering in, neither of them knowing what they were looking at.

Two trucks thundered past, then a car with a lone male driver. None of them stopped.

"I'll put the hazard lights on. Maybe you should try and flash the cars with your T-shirt," Faith said.

Anna glanced down. She was wearing the *Baywatch* top she'd bought in the op shop back in Christchurch. Her hair was pulled back in a messy ponytail and she was sure she must look like a wreck. In Auckland she wouldn't have left the house without makeup but she somehow felt more like herself like this. Like the Anna she used to be when she'd been at tech in Hamilton, before she'd met Greg.

They'd broken down next to a long flat patchy brown paddock full of large fat black cows. One stood near the wire fence lowing sadly at them.

"I've got no reception at all here," Faith told her.

"Shit."

"Should we walk to the nearest house and use a phone maybe?" Faith suggested. Anna looked down the long straight stretch of road. A fair way down in the distance she could see a lone tin letterbox.

"I guess," she said, thinking ruefully of her heeled boots.

"Maybe we could cut across the field?" Faith suggested, clambering down the verge towards the cow. "Oh, look at its lovely eyes," she called as she leant over the fence to stroke its nose.

"*Blooming heck!*" she yelled, leaping back and landing on her butt, before scrambling to her feet again, bits of grass stuck to the elbows of her jumper.

"Are you okay?" Anna asked, trying not to laugh.

"Electric," Faith panted, pointing at the fence. Anna took in the smudgy brown circle on the seat of her jeans and hoped it was just dirt. She was helping her back up the bank when the sound of a motor caught her attention.

An old mud-encrusted quad bike was coming along the verge towards them. A wiry-looking man in a blue Swanndri with a face of grey scruff sat atop it, gesturing frantically at them. He appeared to be yelling but it wasn't until he pulled up beside them and cut the engine that she could hear what he was shouting.

"... leaving your rubbish and your poop and thinking you own the whole bloody place," he was saying.

"Sorry?" Anna asked, looking warily at the gun strapped across the rear rack.

"You bloody freedom campers, thinking you can just park up anywhere, I'm sick of it."

"Oh, we're not ..." Faith started but he cut her off.

"I've a good mind to take care of things the old-fashioned way," he said, reaching back to touch the rifle. "You're lucky I don't. But I've called the police, and I suggest you not be here when they arrive, if you know what's bleeding good for ya!"

"Look, we've broken down ..." Anna started, but he was gunning the quad bike back to life, and then he was off, skidding around and flinging a layer of dirt and dust in their faces before she had a chance to finish, finger raised at them as he went.

"Blooming heck," Faith said again. They looked at each other in disbelief. "What on earth will we do if he comes back?"

"Run?" Anna said with a grimace. "But seriously, I doubt that guy would really shoot us, but I'd rather not take the chance."

They stood looking at the engine again, as if by some miracle one of them may have discovered some hidden mechanical talent.

"Is that thing supposed to be attached to that?" Faith

asked, pointing at a long tube.

"I dunno. But I'm pretty sure that tank thing shouldn't be empty either," Anna said.

She reached back into her pocket and checked her phone again. Unsurprisingly, there was still no service.

"Maybe we need to get some elevation," she said. They both looked around them at the flat grassy plains. There was no hill in sight.

"Perhaps if we got up on the roof?" Faith suggested.

"Oh yes, that might be worth a shot. Shall I boost you up?" Faith looked a little dubious.

"Maybe I should boost you instead? I'm in a skirt and you're taller ..."

"All right," Anna conceded. She slid open the side door and stepped up to stand on the floor inside, reaching up to hold the roof railing. "Just kind of push my bum up, and I'll try to get leverage with my arms a bit."

They heaved and grunted and Anna managed to get one arm up to hold the base of the loo and then Faith pushed until she got a knee over the top. Anna lay panting for a minute, glad the cement had held.

"Bloody hell, I'm nowhere near as fit as I thought I was," she grumbled. "Okay, can you give me a leg up for the final bit?"

Eventually she managed to get herself to the roof, and she stood unsteadily, fishing for her phone.

"Bugger, I broke another nail," she said, inspecting her

French polish. "But I've got one bar," she announced excitedly. "Hey, there's that mate of Baz, in the red car," she said, waving her arms wildly as the Mazda drove past them. "Bugger, I don't know if he saw us."

The car kept going down the road, but it did seem like perhaps he'd slowed for a minute.

"Maybe stand on the loo?" Faith said. "That will make you higher."

Anna looked suspiciously at the old porcelain bowl. There was a large crack from the cistern to the seat and it was far from evenly mounted.

"It's on a bit of a lean. I might slide off and break my neck."

"Well, maybe get on your knees on it," Faith asked hopefully.

"Yeah, maybe."

She sat down carefully on the wonky seat, testing its durability, one arm raised with her phone in hand just as the red car came back towards them. It did a U-turn and slowed to pull in behind them. It seemed about to come to a stop when a police cruiser pulled up behind it. The driver of the Mazda suddenly gunned the engine, pulling back out onto the highway with a pelt of gravel.

"Darn it," Faith said, hands on hips as she squinted after him. "Do you think he got scared off by the cop? Maybe he still thinks we have the drugs."

A car door slammed shut. "Having some trouble, ladies?"

Anna turned towards the police officer. He looked to be

in his mid-forties. He obviously still kept himself in shape judging by the way his uniform clung to his thighs and his shirt fitted tightly over his biceps. His face was handsome, dark eyes with short dark hair, lightly peppered with grey, and a sharp jawline. “Can I help you with anything?

“We didn’t poo anywhere,” Anna blurted out. “Not even in the loo. It’s not real. Well, I mean it is, but not, like, usable ...” She trailed off while he stared silently up at her, lip twitching.

She slid down the side of the van as elegantly as she could, letting go with a little ‘oof’ as she landed on the ground. Her T-shirt had ridden up and she tugged it back down self-consciously.

“Was the Mazda driver a friend of yours?” he asked.

“No. I think he was after the drugs but then he saw you ... I mean ... not *our* drugs, his drugs,” she stuttered incoherently. Jesus Christ. Seeing a hot man seemed to turn her into a blundering idiot. How long had it been since she’d had sex anyway? And why was she thinking about sex right now? “I swear we’re not, like, doing some kind of deal ...” She felt her face flush and fell silent.

“Our van broke down,” Faith interjected helpfully. “I think the guy in that car was going to help us but maybe he thought there was something he didn’t want you to find.” She reached over and gave Anna’s arm a sympathetic pat.

“Officer Kurt Baker,” he said to Faith. He glanced back over at Anna and his mouth twitched like he was trying to hide a smile. He didn't look like he was thinking about having sex with her though, she thought, as he strode over to look under Rizzo's bonnet. Anna wasn't looking at his trousers, pulled tight over his arse. She really wasn't.

"I'll call a towie, I don't think you're going anywhere in a hurry. We can get you into Bode and get someone to have a look at her if you like?"

"Oh, thank you, that sounds good," Faith said.

Anna remained silent.. A small giggle escaped as she thought to herself 'you have the right to remain silent…' and Officer Baker gave her a puzzled look. He probably thought she was on drugs. She wondered whether she should offer to take a saliva test.

"Okay then." He strode to his car and made the call.

"It'll be ten minutes or so. If you ladies would like to wait in my car I'll give you a ride into town."

"Oh, I've never ridden in a police car before," Faith said. "That's a good thing right?"

"I got picked up going to a fancy dress party with a friend once," Anna said as they took their handbags from the van and crossed to the police car. "The officer offered to drive us since we were dressed like French maids and she was worried we wouldn't make it safely."

"Well, God bless the New Zealand police force."

"Indeed," Anna replied. She hadn't realised that Kurt had moved to his car with them. He opened the car door and indicated inside.

"Mind your head," he said as she ducked inside.

Faith got into the other side and leant over to Anna. "Do you think we could take a selfie? The kids would just about die, I think."

"Yeah, and do you think we could persuade Officer Hottie to pose with us?"

Faith giggled. "He is rather dreamy, isn't he? I think he liked your T-shirt too."

"What do you mean?" Anna squawked.

"Well, he was trying to act professional but he looked a bit embarrassed when I caught him looking."

Anna huffed. Faith was probably imagining things.

◇

When Kurt had talked to the towie, who he explained was his cousin Mike, he drove them into Bode. It was a small town, about ten kilometres from where they'd broken down. The streets were wide and quiet, lined with old lantern-style lamps. The houses and shops lining it had painted wooden porches, and tables and chairs dotted the sidewalks. It was rather quaint and charming. They pulled up in front of a corrugated iron building, painted bright blue with large black lettering proclaiming it to be 'Baker's Garage and Towing'.

"My dad's business," he explained. "I'm not showing favouritism, it's the only one in town."

They climbed out of the car. Faith rather reluctantly. Anna thought she'd seemed to enjoy her brief brush with the law.

They should have asked him to put on the siren.

A large black lab came rushing out of the mechanics bay barking furiously until he saw Kurt and then he ran to greet him, tail wagging furiously.

"Hey, King," Kurt said fondly, giving him a vigorous pat.

Anna crouched down and held out her hand. "Hello, gorgeous boy," she cooed and received a wet lick in her ear for her efforts. "Oh, he's beautiful," she said.

Kurt gave her a contemplative look.

"He's not usually so friendly to strangers," he said. "He's more of a guard dog." His tone was a little miffed, like she'd done something to bewitch him, and she shrugged.

"Dogs just always like me," she told him with a grin and then proceeded to smooch King who rubbed up against her like a cat in heat, panting delightedly.

"Anyway, there's a coffee shop just down the road if you want to grab something to eat or drink. Mary does the best cheese rolls I've ever had. Mike shouldn't be too long and I'll get Cliff to have a look and he can tell you what he thinks when you get back." He looked at his watch. "Maybe give him half an hour or so?"

They thanked him and headed in the direction he'd indicated, passing a pharmacy, a beauty salon and a newsagent before coming to the cafe. Old-fashioned lace curtains covered half the large front window and a sign outside said 'Duncan's Doughnuts – open, come on in'. Anna pushed open the hot-pink-painted door and stepped inside to be assaulted by the welcome smell of fresh coffee and icing sugar. It was a smell she remembered from visiting the bakery when she was a child. Her brother used to tease her because she'd spend ages deciding whether to get a custard square or a cream bun. She'd always end up choosing the cream bun. Her mouth watered now at the memory.

"Ooh, lamingtons. And look at all those doughnuts," Faith said, approaching the counter. The vinyl curtain from the kitchen flapped and an older woman stepped out. She shuffled painfully towards the counter.

"Don't mind me, hurt my back," she said. "What can I get you, ladies?"

"I'd love a pot of tea and one of those maple walnut doughnuts, if it's no trouble," Faith said.

Anna ordered a coffee and decided to try one of the famous cheese rolls.

"It's no trouble at all, always lovely to have new faces. What brings you into town?"

Faith explained about the breakdown and that they were passing time while their van was being looked at.

"Cliff is the best. Well, his is the only garage in town but he's also the best. I'm Mary Duncan by the way."

They took a seat near the window. Anna thought it was a shame the curtain blocked the view from the road but she liked the old-fashioned Formica tables. Laminated menus were propped up between a cheery pot of red gerberas and a pink-painted box containing cutlery and paper napkins.

After a great amount of time, Mary shuffled over with their drinks. She walked slowly back to get their food. Anna feared her coffee would be cold by the time she returned.

"Sorry for the delay. I had a girl who was helping me out but she had to return to uni last week. Haven't got round to putting up the 'Help wanted' sign yet but I'm not holding out much hope. I probably should think about selling up and retiring one of these days, I guess."

Faith picked up a magazine from a rack and flipped through it while she sipped her tea. Anna watched Mary as she grimaced while wiping down one of the tables. The door jangled and a young woman with a toddler in a buggy came in.

"Afternoon, Mary, how's the back?"

"Not getting much better, lovey. The physio says I need to take it easy but that's not going to happen now that Gemma's gone. Still, can't complain – although that seems to be all I have been doing," she said with a laugh.

"Can I trouble you for a coffee? A large flat white, please, and one of your little pink doughnuts with the sprinkles for Charlie?"

"Of course, my darling." Mary straightened up and winced and Anna found herself practically leaping up from her seat. "Let me help you," she said. "I know my way round a coffee machine, though I haven't used a commercial one for years."

Mary looked at her with surprise. "I couldn't do that. You're a customer."

"It'll be fun," Anna said in what she hoped was a convincing manner. She was already making her way to the back of the shop. "Here, I'll have it ready in no time. Double shot for your large size, Mary?" She didn't give Mary a chance to protest but gave her hands a quick wash and started the process of making the coffee, added a little fluffy for Charlie with the leftover foamed milk and popped one of the small iced doughnuts onto a plate.

"I'll do the till later," Mary said as the woman handed Anna the correct change. "And thank you so much."

Anna returned to her coffee with a grin. "These really are the best rolls," she said.

"I might give you my secret recipe, if you come back for breakfast." Mary laughed and went over to talk to her new customer.

"Speaking of breakfast, where are we going to stay tonight?" Faith asked, as she took a bite of her doughnut. Each bite she'd taken she'd closed her eyes in ecstasy, as if it was the best thing she'd ever eaten. "I'm getting a bit short of cash."

"I will be soon too," Anna admitted. "I'm going to have to budget for who knows how long until I get hold of a lawyer and get things sorted with Greg. We'll have to pay for the van repairs too. Hopefully this Cliff guy will be able to sort it out quickly and we might be able to find a campground for the night."

◇

There was a bigger problem than they could have anticipated.

"Well, looks like it could be the turbo stepper motor," Cliff told them, wiping his greasy hands on a rag. "I can get a better picture in the morning but I think I'm going to have to get a part from the city. It's likely gonna set you back about three hundred bucks. I can ring around and see if I can find one a bit cheaper though."

Kurt was leaning against an old muscle car in the engine bay listening. Anna had been surprised to see that he was still there. There was a strong resemblance. Cliff must have been in his late seventies but still moved about easily and was handsome in a worn kind of way.

"I can give you a ride to a motel for the night. The Paradise Inn is just down the road – it's clean and pretty good value – but if you want something fancier there's a really nice B&B just out of town," Kurt said.

"The motel sounds like it might be best," Anna told him. "It would be better to be close by. We can't exactly ask you to run us around town in the morning, can we?"

Kurt opened his mouth to say something, then closed it, opened it again and said; "The Paradise is walking distance, but it's on my way home. I'd be happy to take you and you can check it out."

"I'm locking up for the night," Cliff said. "Do you need anything out of the van? It'll be safe here in the yard with King here, but I'll give you the keys so you can come back for your bags if you decide to check in. If you come by in the morning, I'll have made some phone calls about the part."

King was busy leaning against Anna with lovesick eyes and making groaning noises as she rubbed his ears. Anna gave him a kiss on the head as they left and he hung his head sadly. They got back in the patrol car and pulled on their belts. It smelt nice, like vanilla. Kurt got into the driver's seat and peered round at them through the mesh partition.

"So, where are you ladies from?"

"Hawke's Bay for me. Anna's in Auckland," Faith told him. "We just met in Wellington a week ago though."

He gave them a curious look and then turned and started the car, pulling out onto the main road.

"I don't suppose we could turn the siren on, could we?" Faith asked, making Anna laugh loudly. She saw Kurt's face in the rear-vision mirror and he was grinning. He caught her eye and a weird bolt of energy went through her. Lust, she realised with shock. When was the last time she'd felt that? She blushed. The poor man was probably married with four kids and the last thing he was feeling was any kind of lust for her. She kept her eyes on the scenery as they drove through the town, feeling like a fool.

◇

Kurt dropped them at the motel and left. They stood in the front, neither of them making a move to go inside. Faith had been googling to see if they had vacancies on booking.com and looked up at Anna. "It's $179 for the night," she said, worry lines creasing her forehead.

"You know," Anna said slowly, "we could still stay in the van."

"How do you mean?"

"Well, it's just sitting in the yard. We could use the public toilet at that park over the road for the loo and to brush our teeth. We've still got snacks so we could have them for dinner, if you're happy with that?"

"That actually makes sense. We've got perfectly good beds just sitting there for free and I'm not that hungry after the doughnut anyway."

Anna would have to disagree about the perfectly good beds but she was as happy as Faith was to save a bit of money.

◇

It was dusk and the town was quiet. The main street shops had closed up for the night and the only sounds were the odd dog barking and, far in the distance, a morepork. They wandered back to the garage and pulled open the steel framed gate. It rolled open, the catch clanking against the wire mesh. King came out growling deep in his throat, looking a bit menacing in the evening's fading light until Anna called out to him and he bounded towards them with a delighted whine. She gave him a pat as Faith closed up the gate.

"Man, you'd never find a place unlocked like this in Auckland," she whispered.

"I feel like a burglar," Faith whispered back.

"I know. Me too."

They crept across the lot with exaggerated mincing steps, trying not to laugh, King pressed to Anna's side. The van door protested loudly as they slid it open and Anna pulled it carefully shut behind her with a gentle snick. King had gone back to his kennel where he could keep watch over the lot. It was too early to sleep, so they sat on the beds and ate mixed nuts and drank warm iced tea and talked.

"You haven't said much about your husband," Faith said after a bit. "And I'm not sure I should ask?"

Anna thought of brushing things off. She'd gotten used to being vague with friends and family about her marriage, saying 'Oh, we're fine, after twenty-odd years you can hardly expect us to still be madly in love.' But the truth was she was starting to think that not only wasn't she in love with her husband, but that she really didn't even like him very much.

"Things are definitely over there," she told Faith. "They have been for years if I'm honest. I guess I was just biding my time, and it was easier to leave things as they were than make a break and start again. It's a bit scary, change. But I think I'm starting to realise that I'm also excited about that."

Faith gave her a smile.

"I know what you mean. When I left the community, I was so afraid that I'd regret it. That I'd find the grass wasn't greener, you know?"

"Yeah, but you're glad you did leave, right?"

"Absolutely."

"I think this trip has been great actually. It's made me think about who I was, who I've become, who I want to be." She laughed. "Gawd, that's a bit philosophical for a Tuesday night without a drink, isn't it?"

Faith gave her a warm smile. "Maybe, but I'm glad we've done this. It's been a long time since I've had so much fun. And I hope we stay in touch after all this too."

"Oh definitely," Anna agreed.

"I can't be bothered to brush my teeth," Anna confessed.

"Me neither. But I bet I'll have to have a wee in the night."

They jostled around in the back getting on pyjamas and then got into bed.

They lay in the dark, and it felt comfortable, peaceful even. A car drove past slowly then picked up speed after King started to bark. Maybe she could get a dog now, Anna thought. She thought about her marriage, about being on her own, about the possibility of dating again. The image of Kurt came to mind. She imagined what it would be like to kiss another man, to kiss him. He had lovely lips, full and wide, and she imagined what it would be like, breathing him in.

"Would it be bad to have another doughnut for breakfast?" Faith asked suddenly. "Because that was seriously one of the best things I've ever eaten."

Chapter fifteen

The next morning Anna woke when Faith slid back the door of the van, the pale morning light dappling her pillow.

"Sorry," Faith whispered. " I have to pee."

King came snuffling over, tail wagging with delight.

"Hello, beautiful boy."

Anna could swear he was smiling as he settled down next to the door with a contented sigh.

The air was cool, fresh, like you only get in a small town. She burrowed into her bedding and lay thinking about what would need to be done when this trip was over. Going back to the house, packing up her things. She realised there was very little she missed. Photos of the kids, a favourite painting, a few knick-knacks. But the rest all felt so unimportant. All the nice clothes and the jewellery, shoes and handbags. She did want her kitchen things though. Her KitchenAid mixer, her chef's knives that had been a gift for her twenty-first.

Her grandmother's cookbook.

She thought about Faith and her doughnut breakfast and how much Mary's shop reminded her of her gran. Her stomach rumbled and her bladder protested, so she got up, pulled on her sweater and shuffled to look out the van door where King sat up for a pat. It was still very early, and the only person around was a jogger, dressed in tight shorts and a long-sleeved top, his feet echoing on the footpath as he ran past. Faith emerged from over the road, scuttling furtively back in the gate in her striped pyjama pants, arms crossed to still her wayward boobs. Anna grinned. It felt like it might be a good day.

◇

Duncan's Doughnuts was open according to the sign, but Mary was nowhere to be seen inside the cafe. There was a fair bit of clattering and banging from the back though and after hovering for a beat, Anna decided to stick her head in.

"Mary?" she called out, "it's Anna, from yesterday." Mary was in a large industrial-looking kitchen, at odds with the front of the shop. Baked goods lined the stainless steel centre bench and Mary was awkwardly attempting to retrieve a tray of biscuits from a long floor oven, wincing and crouching oddly. Anna took a tea towel from the table and went to help.

"Oh, thank you, darlin'," Mary said, straightening slowly and pointing at a gap on the bench. Anna set the tray down and looked around. There were unfilled doughnuts and a piping bag of custard cream, square sponges and coconut in bowls, and croissants ready to be filled with chicken and Brie. Mary's hair had come loose from her bun and sat lopsided in her hairnet. She looked frazzled.

"Where shall I start?" Anna asked with a grin. Mary gave her an appraising look.

"I'm serious," Anna told her. "Put me to work and pay me with breakfast."

"You, my darling, are an angel," Mary told her. "Make us all a coffee and I'll give you a rundown."

◇

Anna finished off pastries, loaded pies into the warmer and whipped up a batch of cupcakes. Faith helped Mary make hot drinks and do the till and they made it through the breakfast rush. It was surprisingly busy for a small town, Anna noted, as she placed the cupcakes into the front cabinet. She hadn't had this much fun in years, she realised. Mary had given them a running commentary on all the local gossip, and she was truly grateful for their help.

At one point Kurt came into the bakery for a takeaway coffee, looking surprised to see them there helping out and she gave him an awkward wave, her face heating when she thought of where her mind had gone last night. He gave her a funny look and then smiled. Later, she caught herself in the stainless fridge door and realised she had a big smear of chocolate icing across her cheekbone.

After they'd cleaned up the kitchen and cleared the tables,

she and Faith sat and had bacon and egg rolls and hot drinks.

"Well, I suppose we'd better go and check on Rizzo," Anna said, putting their cups into the dishwasher and setting it to go. Mary came up and gave her a long, warm hug, then did the same to Faith.

"I can't thank you girls enough."

"No, it was nothing. Honestly. We had nothing else to do."

"It wasn't nothing. It was everything, truly."

Anna gave her another hug and they set off back to the garage.

◇

Mike was working on a car in the garage and King came to greet them and led them back to Cliff who was on the phone in the office. Elvis crooned about heartache in the background. Anna knocked on the door frame and he looked up, gesturing for them to come in.

"All right, yep. No, fair enough. I know how it is, yep. Okay, see you this arvo." He hung up and wrote some figures down on his desk blotter.

"How are you ladies this morning?" he asked.

"Good, thanks."

"Sleep okay at Paradise?"

"Yes, yes, great. Thanks." Anna avoided looking at Faith in case they looked guilty. Cliff gestured at the chairs in front of his desk and they sat. King placed his head on Anna's lap and she stroked his velvety ears.

"Well, I've got good news and bad news," he told them. "Good news is I've located a part. A second, so it's cheaper. Bad part is, it's in Invercargill and I have to go get it myself." He took a sip from a coffee cup with the words 'STARTER FLUID' printed on it and grimaced. "Green tea," he said with disgust. "Supposed to be good for you, make you live longer, but I'm not sure I want to if this is all I get."

Anna laughed. "It's better with honey," she told him.

"Anyhoo, I was planning to head down in any case this week to see my brother, so I can pick it up no prob, but I won't be back till Sunday at the earliest." He gave them an apologetic grimace. " He's in a home, and he's not so good. I need to go, spend a little time – you know?"

"Oh, I'm so sorry," Faith said.

"Ah no, it is what it is. Old age sucks. But I'm afraid I don't have a courtesy car or anything like that to offer you. So you'll be stuck here for a bit."

"Oh right. Actually, I wonder if we could get a ride with you?" Faith asked. "It's just that I need to get to Invercargill for my brother's birthday on Saturday."

"Oh sure," Cliff said, but he was frowning. "Not a problem, no, that's fine. But I'll be in my ute, so only room for one, I'm sorry."

Faith looked worriedly at Anna who did a mental run through of her finances in her mind. If she put aside the repair money and stayed in the van and didn't bother with lunch, she'd be okay.

"No, you should go," she told Faith. "Absolutely. You need to. I can stay here. It's not a problem." Faith didn't look convinced. "Honestly, I'll be fine."

"I'll have to set off shortly though, if that works for you?" Cliff took another sip of his drink and then pushed it away. "Bugger it, I need a coffee. I might just pop into the cafe and get one for the road. Can I get you ladies anything?"

They declined and he called to King who paused to look at Anna before he eventually followed him down the road. Anna and Faith went over to the van to get Faith's things.

"Are you sure it's okay if I go?" Faith said. "I feel bad. What are you going to do till we get back?"

"Seriously, I'll be fine. Go. Tell me all about it when you get back."

◇

Cliff came back with a drink tray in one hand and a bag with several doughnuts in the other. He had a smudge of flour on his collar.

"Mary tells me you earnt these," he told them, handing over two iced teas. "She's very thankful for the help with her back out an' all."

"Perhaps I'll wander down and see if she needs any help with the lunch rush," Anna said, and Cliff gave her a large smile.

"That would be good of you, lass."

Faith put her bag and the wrapped artwork of Red's she'd bought for Isaac in the cab of his ute and Cliff gave King the nod to get in the back. He looked back and forward from Cliff to Anna.

"What's wrong with you?" Cliff said to him. "Get up." King leapt onto the flat bed and lay down, giving Anna a sorrowful look. She kissed his nose and gave his head a rub.

"Just have to stop real quick and get my bag, and we'll hit the road," Cliff told Faith, who hugged Anna and got into the passenger side door.

"I want to hear all about the palace, and the corgis," Anna told her with a smile. Cliff looked baffled.

"I'll give you a rundown on the way," Faith told him with a laugh.

◇

Anna drank her tea as she wandered back towards the main shops. Maybe she'd splurge on a book, she thought, and laughed to herself at the idea that a book was now a luxury.

Her phone rang. It was Greg. Again. She'd been avoiding his calls while she and Faith had been driving, but she answered this time with a sigh.

"Hi."

"What the hell is bloody well going on with you?" he started. "I'm trying to be patient, Anna, but enough's enough. When the hell are you going to give up this strop and get home? I've got major clients coming Friday and a bloody wife in the middle of some ridiculous mid-life crisis."

Anna laughed quietly to herself. She had no intention of

working any longer on the marriage, but she was still a little stunned at how she'd managed to drag things out this long with a husband whose first thought when his wife left him was for his clients.

"Greg," she said softly, "you need to listen to what I'm saying ..."

"I am bloody listening but you don't seem to realise that ..."

"*I wasn't finished.*" She wasn't yelling really, just talking loud enough to stop him in his tracks for a minute. "I. Am. *Not.* Coming. Back," she said firmly. "I'm done. *We* are done. This is the end of the road. I won't make you sell the business, or the house if you don't want, but I want a fair payout. I'm entitled to it. From now on, I'll be talking to you through my lawyer."

There was an eerie silence and then Greg was off – shouting and cursing. Anna waited patiently for him to finish, her phone away from her ear. When he ran out of steam, she said: "I'm sorry you feel that way, Greg. I wish you well." And then she hung up the phone.

Chapter sixteen

Southland Times:

MUCH ANTICIPATED PALACE GRAND OPENING A ROYAL SUCCESS

The opening night of the much anticipated Buckingham Palace Museum was a star-studded event with more glamour than the Grammys.

Invercargill couple Keith and Isaac Williams finally opened the doors to their homage to the British monarchy on Saturday night in a combined event to celebrate Isaac's fiftieth birthday. The six-year building project was finished just before Christmas and can only be described as a labour of love. The final product, a small-scale replica of Queen Elizabeth's royal London residence, even features a throne room where visitors can take a 'selfie' and has a delightful museum of royal collectables including a dress that belonged to Diana, Princess of Wales.

Keith, a well-known local businessman, has been a royalist since he was a teen and has amassed an impressive amount of memorabilia over the years.

All Blacks Corey Flynn and Anton Oliver, actor Marton Csokas and singer Suzanne Prentice all attended, with Mayor Tim Shadbolt making an impressive opening speech.

Entry to the museum is $10 and well worth every penny if only for a glimpse of the fantastic art that Keith commissioned from local artist Greg Macdonald.

Cliff wasn't much of a talker and after giving him a quick rundown on her brother and his castle, Faith found herself dozing off soon after they'd left town. She had a strange dream about her childhood — or perhaps it wasn't a dream, more a memory. When she was about seven she'd gone fishing in the creek on their property with Isaac and her next sister up, Charity. She and Charity had hitched their long dresses up into their voluminous underpants — an absolute sin if anyone had seen them. Faith had felt an eel brush against her leg and Isaac had hoisted her up onto his back and piggybacked her safely to the riverbank.

When Isaac had left home a year or so later, Faith hadn't understood why. She remembered feeling bereft and abandoned. Nobody was allowed to mention his name and even when she tried to ask her mother where he was and why he'd gone when her father wasn't home, her mother had frowned and hushed her. It wasn't until years later, just before Faith had left for Christchurch to start her nursing, that Charity had told her about the rumour. Her husband, Jebediah, had been in Invercargill. Isaac was living there with a man. At the time, Faith hadn't believed it. Why would a man live with another man? It wasn't until she had been exposed to more of the world that she'd thought it could be possible. Isaac's sudden departure from the community, his refusal to consider marrying any of the girls the elders had suggested for him. And then it was like he'd never existed.

◇

Cliff brought her out of her reverie by offering her one of the doughnuts from the bag. She selected a filled raspberry one and munched it happily.

"Did Bev not give you any breakfast this morning?" he asked, deftly sipping his coffee and negotiating a tight bend in the road.

"Bev?" Faith said, puzzled.

"At the Paradise. She normally sets out some of Mary's doughnuts and a pot of coffee for the guests."

Faith felt her cheeks flush. She thought about making up a story, but she'd never been a very good liar.

"Oh, um, actually, we didn't stay at the motel. It was a little bit out of our budget so we went back to the van for the night. I hope you don't mind, seeing as it was parked in your yard."

"You should have said. It doesn't bother me at all but I could have left you access to the kitchen and toilet. Lucky King took a liking to your friend, huh? He'd probably have been barking all night otherwise. Will Anna be there tonight as well?"

"Yes, is that okay?"

"No skin off my nose. Just send her a message on your phone and tell her there's a key hanging under the hose box next to the office, got a yellow plastic tab. That will let her get into the building after Mike's closed up."

Faith dutifully pulled out her phone to text Anna.

"Did you say your brother was in care, Cliff?"

"Yeah, has been for a few years now. Parkinson's."

"Oh, that's tough."

"Yeah. He was an electrician. Started getting tremors and whatnot in his fifties. Had to retire eventually. He's pretty bad now. Been in a wheelchair for about a year, and now he's got a chest infection, pneumonia maybe."

"Oh, that's no good."

"No, but he still mostly knows who we all are, which is good. Means we can say goodbye, you know?"

Faith thought about that as they drove, about her brother and sisters and their relationship to each other. She was so glad she was making this trip to see Isaac, and had the chance to build up their connection again.

◇

They arrived in Invercargill well before lunch and Faith got Cliff to drop her at the shops so she could pick up some flowers. She had rung Keith and arranged for him to pick her up, so she gave Cliff an awkward side hug and a thank you and waited for her brother-in-law to arrive.

He pulled up in a beautifully restored red 1980s Rolls-Royce and got out with a huge grin on his face. He was in his sixties, with salt and pepper hair and wire-rimmed glasses. He had on checked golf pants and a striped jumper with a bright-pink triangle on the front.

"Oh, my Lord, you look so much younger than I was expecting," he told her. "I've been looking at your crusty old brother too long." He laughed as he hugged her. "He is going to die when he sees you."

"So he really doesn't know I'm coming?" Faith asked. She was a bit nervous to see Isaac, she realised.

"Not a clue. He'll be so thrilled. Come on, jump in Margaret and we'll go surprise him at home."

◇

The castle was about twenty minutes from the city just off the main road. They drove through wrought iron gates and down a beautiful shell-lined driveway that crunched under the tyres. Keith gave a running commentary the whole way about the construction and the grand opening.

"The crest for the gates was wrong, so it's gone back. The guy promised it would be done by this afternoon so fingers crossed. The people are coming this afternoon to set up a marquee so Isaac won't be surprised I'm home. I'm normally at golf today."

She wasn't sure what she'd been expecting, but the castle was a shock. It really was a miniature Buckingham Palace. A long off-white stone building with three storeys and a large fountain out front, with an imposing gold centrepiece. Three yapping corgis came rushing from around the side of the house, followed by a man in jeans and gumboots, a large smile on his face at the sight of Keith. Despite the modern clothes, and the receding hairline, he still looked just like the brother she remembered. A lump rose in her throat.

"Hello, love," he called. She watched him as he realised Keith wasn't alone, as the recognition of who she was crossed his face. She stood there, holding the roses awkwardly in front of her, feeling strangely exposed. His hand rose to cover his mouth, eyes wide.

"Oh, my God," he whispered. "Faith?" She nodded. Tears welled up in his eyes and he made a choked sound in his throat. She was vaguely aware of Keith taking their picture on his phone and then Isaac was hugging her, lifting her right off the ground and her heart was bursting out of her chest.

"Oh, my God," he said again. "I can't believe it."

They hugged forever, neither of them wanting to let go first. At their feet the dogs sat, panting and yelping for attention. Eventually they pulled apart and just looked at each other, grinning like loons. The flowers were crushed.

"Hi," Faith said, and they both laughed. "Happy birthday for yesterday. I would have been here sooner, but ... well, it's a long story."

They hugged again. "I can't believe it. This is amazing," Isaac said. They were both crying.

"*Andrew!*" Keith called loudly. "Stop shagging Charlotte, you dirty old bugger." The older dog gave him a mournful look and slunk off across the lawn past a beautifully hedged bed of red poppies.

"This place is incredible," Faith told them. "I can't wait to see inside."

"Yes, let's go in. I have champagne chilling," Keith said, giving Isaac a kiss as he went past. Isaac reached out and took his hand.

"Thank you so much, love," he said, and Keith gave him a look so filled with adoration that Faith felt like she was intruding.

"You're welcome, babe, now let's have a drink before we all start to cry again."

◇

They sat in the formal front room, on gorgeous pale-blue brocade chairs in front of a white and gold fireplace, sipping fancy champagne in Waterford crystal flutes. Keith made a charcuterie board and they nibbled on fancy crackers, salmon and Brie. Faith felt madly underdressed and unworldly until Isaac burped loudly and Keith told him off with a grin.

They talked about the opening night that was happening that Saturday, and about the royals. Keith was most definitely not a Meghan Markle fan and he and Isaac had obviously had numerous disagreements about her in the past.

"All I'm saying, hun, is that sometimes it takes someone like her to stir things up. Nothing wrong with challenging tradition just for tradition's sake."

Keith sniffed. "It's the why though, babe. What's the intention? I'm all for a good stir of the pot, but not just because you can."

"Anyway, we'll have to agree to disagree, as usual," Isaac said. "Tell me, Faith, all about Daniel and the kids? It's Becky's final year at school, right? How did the move into the flat go for Rachel?"

Faith told them about the flat and meeting Anna, then about the van, and the toilet and the incident at the bank. Both men were crying with laughter by the end.

"Oh, my God, Faith, it sounds like you've been having a ball," Isaac said.

"I have. I feel like I'm getting a chance to be a silly teenager," she told him.

"Well, Lord knows we never got to do that," Isaac said. The mood sobered up. "Have you talked to Charity lately?"

"Not since Christmas. And only for a few minutes then."

"Did she tell you about Dad?"

"No? What about him?"

"Oh, well, maybe we should do this later? I feel like I'm

bringing down the mood now."

Faith set down her glass. "What's going on?"

"Shit. Okay, well, fuck. He's dying, Faith. Asbestos poisoning."

Wow. Faith picked up her glass and chugged it back in one hit. Keith refilled it and gave her shoulder a pat.

"Okay, I wasn't expecting that." She thought about her father. All the lecturing and disapproval and indoctrination. And then she thought of all the times he'd played cricket with them on the back lawn, and the little patch of garden he'd allotted her just for flowers. "Right. Well, I guess he'll be thrilled. He'll get his redemption in heaven and all that." She sounded bitter, but the words stuck in her throat. She felt a bit sick.

"You should think about going to say goodbye while you're down here," Isaac said gently.

"What? No. No way."

"Just think about it, Faith. For you, not for him."

"What about you? Do you want to see him?"

Isaac gave her a tight smile. "I tried ringing. Asked to speak to him. I heard him say to Charity that he didn't have a son. So no. I won't be going. But I made my peace with things years ago when I left. I always knew this is how it would be for me with them."

"Bloody hell," Keith complained. "This was supposed to be a happy reunion. Let's not talk about the bloody cult and your sperm donor, shall we? Come on, I'll show you to your room, Faith. I've put you in the Diana quarters. And then we'll have a look at all the photo albums, shall we? While we drink some more bubbles and talk about me."

Faith laughed and gave him a grateful smile. He was a lovely guy, she thought. And they made a fantastic couple. Daniel would love them both. She was missing him, she realised. His calmness and his unwavering support of her. She wondered what he would say about her father being sick. He'd blamed Daniel for corrupting her when they'd finally come clean and tried to resolve things. Daniel had taken it well, and he never bad-mouthed her family, but he'd been adamant that the girls not attend church unless they wanted to go. She wanted to hear his voice, she thought, as she followed Keith up the grand imperial staircase.

◇

Faith lay on the four-poster bed that was a sea of white pillows and rang Daniel. He sounded happy to hear from her like always. He was busy as usual with marking and planning for his classes. She could imagine him sitting at their dining table with his glasses on, hair sticking up at the back from where he always rubbed it when he was concentrating. She felt a surge of affection for him as they talked.

"Well, sweetheart, I'd better go, I promised the favourite child I'd drop her and some mates off at the cinema and then I'm going to meet Jake for a beer."

"Okay, I'll talk to you again tomorrow?"

"Sounds good. Oh, and why don't you see if Tania is around? She's down that way, isn't she?" Faith hadn't seen Tania since she'd quit nursing college, but they'd stayed in touch sporadically via Facebook.

"True. I might flick her a message and see if she's around."

"All right, love you."

"Love you too."

She hung up and lay back thinking about her dad. Daniel had been very neutral about the news of his illness. He'd suggested she go and visit if she thought she needed to see him, but not if it was going to make her feel awful. "It's up to you, hun, do what feels right but do it for you – not for him." But she wasn't sure what felt right, right now.

She composed a quick message to Tania and then dragged herself off her cloud of a bed and went to the bathroom. When she got back, Tania had already replied saying how thrilled she was to hear from her and she would love to catch up. They arranged to meet for coffee the next day, and then Faith went back downstairs to give Isaac his gift, only to be met with the hilarious sight of Keith dressing Charlotte in a Queen's Guard uniform, while Harry ran round in circles trying to remove his Union Jack tutu.

◇

Keith led her into the kitchen where Isaac was standing stirring something at their Aga-style floor oven. The gorgeous aroma of garlic and basil filled the air.

"I thought maybe we'd just eat in here?" Keith suggested, indicating the marble centre island.

"Perfect," Faith agreed. He poured them more drinks and they sat in the warmth of the kitchen where Faith felt far more at home. Despite the modern appliances and expensive fittings, the room had a lived-in feel, with a pile of papers on one end of the bench and a bowl of assorted junk beside it, gardening twine trailing over its edge. On the wall were several framed prints, and Faith realised they were of Isaac and Keith's wedding day. She got back up to have a look at their smiling faces, the stunning backdrop of Coronet Peak behind them.

"I'm so sorry we never made it down for this," she said, feeling so regretful to have not shared in their day.

"No, don't be silly. We totally understood. It was a bad time of year for Dan and money was tight, we got it," Isaac insisted.

"I know, but I'm sort of wishing we'd swallowed our pride and taken you up on the offer to pay. It looks beautiful."

"It was. Perhaps we'll all go again for our tenth anniversary," Keith said.

"I can't believe it was only six years ago," Isaac said.

"Yes, but there were almost twenty before that," Keith pointed out with a laugh.

"I was awful to him when we first got together," Isaac told Faith, and Keith got up to serve the pasta, giving Isaac a playful slap on the shoulder.

"Rubbish," he said. "Don't listen to him, Faith."

"I was though," Isaac told her. "I made him sneak around for so long because I didn't want to be openly gay." He took a sip of his wine and Faith smiled gently at him.

"I was terrified when I left the Servants. I only left because I was left with no real choice." Faith must have looked a little baffled because he gave a sad laugh. "I keep forgetting how little you were. You wouldn't remember." He shrugged. "I kissed Abe Samuels. He was a year above me and I'd had a crush on him forever. But someone told Father and then he was determined to get me straight. Marry me off."

Faith listened sadly, trying to imagine how he must have felt growing up gay in their community.

"You mentioned something before about them trying to get the gay out?" she said tentatively. "Was it awful what they did?"

"Oh no, nothing like they do in America or anything. It wasn't that bad. They just made me sit with the elders, who prayed away my sin, encouraged me to beg forgiveness. Their theory was that if I didn't act on my urges, I could still be redeemed. All they wanted was to marry me off and they could pretend it had been an aberration."

"Still," Faith said. "That must have been terrifying as a teen."

"Yeah. The hardest thing was telling them I was going, really. That I didn't want to be 'fixed'." He gave Faith a grin. "But I just knew I couldn't ever have sex with a girl." He pulled a revolted face and she laughed.

"Me neither," she said and they both cracked up.

"So anyway, I arrived in Invercargill, with no idea what to do and terrified of anyone knowing what a sinner I was. Gradually I sorted out the job, got a flat, eventually immersed myself in normal life, but I didn't dare to tell anyone my sexual orientation."

Keith came back with plates of pasta and a bowl of Parmesan and they tucked in.

"When Keith asked me out the first time, I completely panicked," Isaac said, and Keith smiled fondly at him as he ate. "I turned him down three times before I finally realised that I was being an idiot."

"But then you asked me," Keith said, "and that was very, very brave."

"But I insisted on sneaking around, not admitting we were dating," Isaac said sadly. "And you were out, and proud. It would have seemed like I was ashamed of you. I wasn't," he told Faith. "I was ashamed of myself."

Keith gave him an exasperated look and held his hand over the counter.

"Yeah, I get it," Faith told Isaac. "To some extent anyway. I felt the same about getting pregnant. This is delicious by the way," she said, forking the last mouthful of her dinner into her mouth.

"Well, it was all worth it," Keith declared, "and he's put up with my old bones all this time, so we're even. Now let's have dessert." He got up to clear the plates, waving away their offers of help and went into the scullery to load the dishwasher.

"He's lovely," Faith told Isaac. "And it's lovely to see you two together. You're a gorgeous couple."

"Thanks. I feel very lucky to have him. I don't know how things would have turned out without him in my life." Faith thought again of Daniel and realised she felt lucky to have him too.

"I'm so grateful to have you here, Faith," Isaac told her.

"Me too."

They both looked at each other, teary again. Keith emerged carrying a large cake, took one look at the two of them and started to laugh.

"You two are such softies," he said fondly. "I don't know if we need more alcohol or less?"

"More," they said in unison.

Chapter seventeen

Bode Chronicle:

BEAT THE WINTER BLUES AT BODE BEAUTY

Bode's newly refurbished hair and beauty salon is having a sale.

Come on in and get a spray tan – perfect for the ball season with a free brow tint and shape.

Haircuts and up-dos will also be discounted, so pop in to see Gina and get a conditioning treatment half price for all of this month.

Mother's Day packages including mani/pedi and facials will also be available.

Bode Beauty is open Wednesday through Saturday. Bookings recommended.

Feeling at a bit of a loose end without Faith, Anna wandered down to the cafe to see if she could be of any help to Mary.

"You've already done so much," Mary said. "I couldn't possibly expect you to do anything more."

Mary was clearly struggling. Everything was clean and well organised in the kitchen but it was obvious there was too much work for her on her own.

"I've got nothing to do and nowhere to go for the next few days," Anna told her, tying a rose-printed apron around her waist. "I really don't fancy hanging out in the back of the van or talking to Mike at the garage all day. Seriously, I love this stuff. Let me help."

"All right, but I'm going to pay you, you know. I'd be paying someone to do the work if I could find some help anyway."

Anna thought about refusing, but that was stupid. She needed the money.

"Okay, I can help till Cliff gets back with my car part and fixes the van up."

"I'll pay you in cash if you like? Here, put this on." Mary threw her a hair net and Anna pulled a face but tugged it on and stuffed her long ponytail underneath. She thought a little wistfully of her hairdryer.

While Mary dealt with the last of the morning tea crowd, Anna peeled eggs for sandwiches and made crème anglaise for the custard squares. Being in a commercial kitchen reminded her fondly of her chef school days, and of the part-time job she'd had in a bakery in Hamilton. Her flatmates had loved her when she'd brought home leftover sausage rolls and doughnuts at the end of the day. Hugely helpful when you were on a struggling student budget.

"Do you make salads for lunch, Mary?" she asked, when the older woman brought a stack of dishes back to be washed.

"I probably should. Maybe some of those fancy wrap things too, like you see in the city. Some of the younger ones ask for them, but I'm a bit of a stick-in-the-mud, I'm afraid, and I'm too old to change now."

"It's a lovely cafe. Very homely," Anna said. "Apart from adding a few things like that, I really wouldn't change much about it."

"The older folk like what they like," Mary agreed. "But they took it well when I put in the new coffee machine. A few complained that they missed their filter coffee but even Cliff was ordering a skinny latte within days. Silly old bugger," she laughed. "I'm well ready to retire, but I do love the customers. Some of them have been coming here for years. Some I remember as wee ones bring in their little ones now."

Anna had been introduced to several of the regular customers and had been surprised to find how welcoming they had been of her. She'd gotten so used to Aucklanders with their constant stressed, pressed-for-time attitudes. It was a nice change of pace to chat and not feel the need to rush.

She and Mary worked companionably together and by three had shut the doors. Anna cleaned the kitchen thoroughly while Mary took stock of what she needed to order for the next day. It was nice to do some physical work, Anna realised. She felt industrious, and like she'd accomplished something, even if it was just mastering the deep-fryer to get the glazed doughnuts just right.

"See you tomorrow, I'll be here early," Anna said with a wave as Mary locked up for the day. It was unlikely she'd have a great night's sleep in the van, especially on her own. She was feeling a little bit nervous about being there without Faith, if she was being entirely honest.

Rather than go back to Rizzo too early she crossed the road and walked through the little park, admiring the early autumn colours and neat flower beds, and then wandered back up the main street. The hairdressing salon, Bode Beauty, was still open and the money Mary had paid her was sitting in a wad in her pocket.

It was a more modern shop than the rest on the main road. While most had flowering hanging baskets in their doorways, the hairdressers featured a black lacquered door with a diamante cut-glass doorknob and a sparkly fake chandelier in the entrance where a small counter housed a long glass jar filled with seashells and coloured glass beads. Two women stood chatting by the counter and they didn't look busy, so on a whim, she pulled open the door and went in. The hair net had been awful and she'd felt like Ena Sharples all day. After her talk with Greg that morning, she felt ready for a change.

"Hi," she called tentatively. The two women looked up and the shorter one, with the blue-black pixie cut, gave her a wide smile.

"Hey, come in. What can we do for you?"

"Are you free at the moment for a haircut?" Anna asked.

"Sure, no problem. I was just talking to Tina about the merits of gel nail polish. I'm Gina, by the way." She held out a hand with short polish-less nails for Anna to shake. "Come and take a seat and we'll see what we can do for you. What are you after?"

"Just a cut, I think," Anna said, sinking gratefully into the squishy leatherette chair.

"No colour?" Gina picked up a strand of Anna's hair and ran it through her fingers. "Nice blonde, by the way, you have well-looked-after hair."

Anna sighed. "You know what, I'm kind of sick of the constant highlights and conditioning masks. And the blow-drying. Too much maintenance. Can you cut it all off? I love your cut but I don't know if it would suit me."

"You have a gorgeous face, lovely wide eyes. Any style would look fine but how about we go for a bit longer? Chin-length bob, perhaps with a bit of texture like you've just rolled out of bed and don't give a shit."

Anna laughed. "That sounds perfect. Kind of how I'm feeling right now."

Tina's waxing appointment arrived and she took her to the treatment room at the back of the shop. "Don't go before I get to have a look," she said over her shoulder.

It was nice to have a proper hair wash and Gina gave a great head massage. Anna told her so.

"Thanks, my husband would suggest I could put my strong

fingers to better use." She flexed her fingers and cackled. "Do you think he means opening jars?"

Gina started deftly pinning, combing and cutting and Anna's hair soon lay in long, pale strands on the floor, like the old Anna had just shrugged off her fancy clothes and was now sitting bold and naked. A phoenix rising from the ash.

"You're new in town, aren't you? What brings you here?"

"How do you know I'm new? Do you know everyone here?"

"Pretty much. I grew up here as a kid and now I'm back, not much has changed. One thing about being a hairdresser is that you get to hear all the local gossip. Believe me, some of it I'd really rather not know. Last week, Audrey Graham told me that her husband likes to suck her toes, which is why she gets Tina to give her a pedicure every week. Audrey is about seventy. Not judging, you know, but there are some things you don't need to be privy to." She laughed. "So, what's your story?"

"I'm on a road trip with a friend and our camper broke down," Anna said. "Fortunately we were saved by a very hunky policeman who brought us into town and now we're just waiting to get the van fixed."

"You must mean Kurt. I don't think anyone would have called our other cop, Wayne, hunky for at least twenty years. If ever." She snorted and grinned at Anna's reflection in the mirror.

'He's hot enough to make you want to commit a crime and have him cuff you. I suppose he's married though?"

"Are you digging for information?" Gina laughed. "Kurt's

single. He was married to Julie but they've been divorced for years now. Nice guy too. How's this length for you?"

Anna found she desperately wanted to know more about Kurt but couldn't bring the conversation back round to him without seeming obvious. They talked about which celebrities they thought would hook up and who was going to be next to announce they were pregnant with twins and any chance to find out more about Kurt was lost.

Tina finished with her customer and came out from the back wearing a long zebra print trench coat with a matching handbag. "I'm off. Your hair looks amazing by the way. Are you still on for drinks later, Geens?"

"Sure, six sound good?" She stopped in the middle of scrunching product into Anna's hair. "Hey, you and your friend should come too. Nothing fancy, just a glass of wine at the local pub. They do two for one on a Wednesday night and half-price nachos."

It sounded a lot more appealing than a can of baked beans in the back of Rizzo.

"My friend, Faith, has gone to Invercargill for a few days but if you don't mind me tagging along?"

"Of course not," Gina said.

"The more the merrier," Tina added. "It's just down the road, past the hardware store. O'Leary's."

◇

Anna unlocked the door to the garage, hoping to use the toilet and have a quick wash-up and put some makeup on before she met Gina and Tina at the pub. She was glad, on reflection, that she didn't have to cook in the small staff kitchen, which consisted of an ancient kettle, a dirty microwave and a couple of coffee-stained mugs. There was a Formica table with two wobbly chairs and a seat in the corner with ripped crimson vinyl. It looked like it had come out of the front of a 1960s Morris Minor. The bathroom was worse, with a faded pin-up of a young Britt Ekland, who someone had given a handlebar moustache. Anna cleared a space in the grimy mirror and attempted to put a bit of makeup on. She swapped her T-shirt for her cashmere jumper but didn't bother changing her jeans. She checked that Rizzo was locked, glanced around the yard at the dark shadows and wished King was there.

◇

O'Leary's was warm and crowded. It was a typical Irish pub, darkly lit with a row of beer taps lining the small wooden bar that ran along the back in an L shape. There were round wooden bar leaners and flags on the wall. A fiddle hung above the bar and two slot machines sat against a wall near the bathroom corridor. It smelt faintly of sweat and whiskey and there was a steady thrum of voices. Anna spotted Gina at a table by the window and wandered over to join her.

"Here," she said, pushing a glass of white wine over to her. "Take Tina's drink since she's not here yet. Probably peeling one of the kids off her leg or chewing Mike out about something. Besides, she owes me for last week."

The wine was barely cold and tasted like it had come out of a cask but Anna wasn't complaining. Tina arrived a moment later, throwing off her coat and flopping into a spare seat. There was a splodge of tomato sauce on her pale skinny jeans, marring an otherwise perfect look.

"Bloody hell, you'd think by now Mike would remember Cody only eats plain pasta, wouldn't you?" she sighed. "Oi, where's my drink?"

"Gave it to Anna here. You're too slow."

"I'll get another four then," she said, getting up. "Have to catch up. Nachos as well?"

She was back in no time, having pushed her way to the front of the bar, balancing a table number and four drinks. Men parted like the red sea as she came through and she carefully placed the drinks on the table. "So, are you one of the plumber chicks in the toilet van?" she said to Anna.

"What? No, we're not plumbers. But we are in the van – it's a long story."

"Mike was telling me about towing you and I put two and two together that you were the chick from the salon. Said he'd never seen two such ace-looking plumbers but your van was shit."

"Mike from the garage?"

"Yeah, my husband. His uncle Cliff owns the garage but he's more or less retired. Mike's been there since he left school."

"Hey, you were all over the internet," Gina said suddenly. "There were a whole heap of students tracking you, weren't there? Apparently if someone took a photo, their friends had to shout them a pint or something."

"Should have got Mike to snap a picture then. I could have got you bitches to buy me a wine," Tina sniffed. She'd almost drained her first glass already. "Hey, I have two little monsters," she said when Gina gave her a look. "You've already got Molly off your hands."

Anna was about to ask about husbands and kids when a cheery-looking woman brought over two huge bowls of nachos. She realised she hadn't eaten since breakfast that morning and was suddenly starving.

Someone came around after that selling tickets for a meat raffle and they had another glass of wine before Tina announced she needed to get home. Her youngest, Cory, was only a baby and still liable to wake up a hundred times in the night, she told Anna. Gina declared she needed to get going too as her first customer was booked in for eight-thirty and Anna realised she'd need to be up even earlier to help Mary. They parted ways outside the pub, and Anna made her way back to the garage. Once again, she wished King was there as she pushed open the gate and slunk across the shadowy yard to Rizzo. Without even bothering to remove her makeup, she pulled on pyjamas and climbed into bed. She'd never sleep, she thought, on her own with all the noises of the night.

◇

Shit, she thought, waking some time later. Why hadn't she peed at the pub? It was all very well lying here thinking she'd go back to sleep and her bladder would wait until morning, but she knew it wouldn't. Anna had never been overly afraid of the dark but the car yard freaked her out a little. The tow truck loomed like a menacing Transformer as she trotted across the asphalt, shivering from the cold. She unlocked the door and felt her way along the wall to the dirty bathroom. After she'd peed as quickly as she could, she crept back to the van, eager to get back into her warm bed.

A shadowy figure moved near the van. Anna froze. It was probably nothing. The light was playing tricks. She took a step forward and the shadow moved again. It was definitely a person and it spun towards Anna. She was close enough to see that it was a man, tall, head covered by a beanie. Anna's mouth opened wordlessly. Her feet were glued to the spot. Her heart thumped loudly in her chest. The figure moved towards her, something in his hand, raised above his head, like the grim reaper in a horror movie.

Headlights from a car suddenly lit up the yard and shone on the man too. She could see now that he was holding a crowbar. A car door opened, and then slammed. A choking warbled sound erupted from Anna as relief flowed through her as the man dropped the crowbar, turned and fled, scaling the back fence surprisingly quickly.

"Stop, police," a voice called. "Stay there," he commanded Anna as he took chase. It was Kurt, she realised. He disappeared, clambering over the fence, after her assailant.

Anna wrapped her arms around herself and by the time Kurt came back she was shaking, both with adrenaline and cold. He was panting a little.

"Couldn't catch him. He disappeared in a red Mazda but I got the plates. Are you okay?"

"I'm okay, I think. He was trying to get into the van."

"Any idea who he was?"

Anna shook her head.

"Come on, hop in the car. I'll put the heater on. I'll take you back to my place for a cuppa."

Anna made sure Rizzo was locked and climbed into the police car, suddenly very aware she was only wearing pyjamas. While Kurt went around to the driver's side she took a quick peek in the rear-vision mirror. Her makeup was a complete mess but at least her new haircut still looked pretty good. Kurt opened the driver's door and she quickly sat back, hoping he hadn't seen her checking herself out.

"Nice hairdo," he said. She was sure he was smirking and she wished she could say it wasn't attractive.

"What were you doing down here anyway?" she said, coming off a bit snappy.

"Dad – Cliff – rang me to say you were staying here. Thought I might check to make sure you were okay."

"So you specially came down because you thought I'd be frightened or something?"

"Part of the job," he replied. His smile faltered. "Looks like it was just as well I did."

They didn't speak as Kurt reversed the car and drove a short way before turning into a driveway. It was too dark to see much but Anna could make out a single-level weatherboard house. Kurt led her into a cosy kitchen, not much changed from when it had been built in the 1960s from the look of it. He flicked on a jug and took two mugs down from a cupboard.

"Tea?"

"Thanks."

"Milk? Sugar?"

"Just milk, thanks."

They were silent again until he put a steaming mug of tea in front of her. Anna wrapped her hands around it gratefully. There was a heat pump on in the room and it was warm.

"What were you doing staying in the van anyway?" Kurt asked. "I thought you were at the motel?"

"We were going to, but we're on a bit of a budget. It seemed wasteful when we had free beds just down the road. I'm sorry, we should have just checked with Cliff that it was okay."

"Do you have any idea why someone was trying to break in?"

"You said he got into a red Mazda, right? Well, a red Mazda pulled up just before you rescued us from the roadside yesterday, and then it took off."

"Yes, I remember."

Anna sighed. "I think he was after the drugs."

Kurt raised his eyebrows for just a second before he adopted what she imagined was his professional interrogation face and waited for her to continue.

"I think it might have been the same guy who we saw in Dunedin. He was trying to get into the van when we got back from lunch and said something about knowing the guy we bought it off in Wellington and leaving something behind. Faith thought it was the crappy rap CD in the glove box so she gave him that, but afterwards we thought it might have been the drugs he was after."

"Go on."

"Well, when we bought the van, we found some stuff in a little bag."

"What kind of stuff?

"You know." She lowered her voice. "Cannabis. Weed. Little Green Friends."

Kurt barked out something like a laugh but then it became a cough. "So you think this guy followed you all the way from Wellington for, what, a fifty bag of weed? Maybe if it was a brick of coke ..."

"Oh God, you don't think my ex-husband's got someone following me, do you?"

"Does he want you dead?" She was sure his lips twitched again.

"It does seem a bit unlikely. He's a dickhead but he's a bit squeamish."

"But you think he might have you followed?"

"Well, only because I've left him."

"So do you still have the weed?"

"No, we, er, burnt it."

"You smoked it?"

"No! God, no. We threw it in a fire. We didn't mean to inhale any of it."

Kurt kept his mug up by his face but his eyes were smiling. "Okay, so we've established you no longer have it. Is there anything else you've found in the van that someone might have wanted?"

"Nothing at all. Definitely not the budget brand baked beans."

Anna finished her tea. "I guess I'd better get back. I'm helping Mary out tomorrow and want to get there by six if I can."

"You're not going back down there."

"Like I said before, I can't really afford the motel at the moment. I've still got to sort the finances from my split with my ex-husband."

"We've no idea whether the guy will come back and he was clearly willing to assault you earlier. You can stay here. We've got a spare room."

"We?" She felt a moment of disappointment. Gina must have got it wrong that Kurt was single.

"I live with my dad."

"Oh. Right." Now it was her turn to raise her mug up to cover her grin.

"Come on, I'll show you to the room."

Kurt led Anna down a hallway. She wondered which room was his but all the doors were shut, apart from one which was clearly the bathroom. He pushed open a door and switched on the light, holding the door for her to enter. "Sorry, it's just a single but probably more comfortable than the van anyway. Bathroom's across the hall, there are towels in the cupboard under the sink." His eyes roved over her pyjamas briefly. "I can take you back to the van in the morning and we'll pick up your stuff but you'd be best to stay here until Cliff gets back with your part. I'll leave something for you to wear in the morning outside the door."

"Thank you."

He left, closing the door behind him, and Anna looked around. There was a bed against the wall, a chest of drawers next to it and a straight-backed chair in the corner. No other furniture. Two posters were pinned to the wall – the one above the dresser was an '80s band picture of Guns N' Roses and another, right beside the bed, of Pamela Anderson. A framed photo on the dresser showed a teenaged Kurt standing proudly next to a grey Ford Escort. This must be Kurt's childhood bedroom, she thought as she climbed into bed, pushing the naughty thoughts that suddenly surfaced deep down into the recesses of her mind.

It took her a little longer to get to sleep this time thinking about Kurt in the next room, but when she did, it was for the same reason.

Chapter eighteen

The next morning Anna got up with the sun and had a welcome shower, relishing the hot water and Kurt's body wash. It smelt like him, woody with a hint of bourbon. He'd left her a pair of sweats that she rolled at the top and a navy sweatshirt that hung down over her hands. She would definitely need to go back to Rizzo for clothes before she headed to the bakery. Especially since she had no underwear on, which made her feel surprisingly sexy in his clothes.

Kurt was up, despite the early hour, and was leaning against the kitchen counter drinking a protein shake, dressed in running shorts and a long-sleeved, tight compression shirt.

"Hungry?" he asked, and she had to look up from where she was ogling his thighs.

"What? No, I was just ..." He gave her an odd look.

"I'm just going to jump in the shower. If you want coffee or anything, help yourself. Then I'll give you a ride back to the garage, yeah?"

Do not imagine him in the shower – naked, Anna thought with a gulp. It felt unseasonably warm all of a sudden, and all she could do was nod. 'Get a grip,' she told herself. 'You're not bloody sixteen.'

Even so, she snooped around his house like a teenager while he got ready. It was comfy, lived in, with the lingering smell of orange wood polish. The lounge had two sofas, a thick rug and a coffee table as well as a beautiful sideboard. Framed pictures covered the surface. There was one of a very young and handsome Cliff outside a church with his bride, a family shot with the two of them and two small boys, one of Mike and Cliff outside the garage, and one of a younger Kurt at what looked like his police graduation, his arm around another smiling guy with large ears and a ginger buzz-cut. No sign of his wedding photo, she noted.

Out the back door was a large newish deck, with a barbecue, table and chairs and pots of herbs. Behind it was a long expanse of lawn and beautiful established gardens. A long row of camellias lined the end where a beehive sat. It was gorgeous and Anna slipped out and wandered barefoot on the dewy lawn to take a better look. Her feet went numb almost instantly, but it was like a little oasis, tranquil and fragrant with two swallows flitting from the eaves of the house. Anna let out a contented sigh.

"It was my mum's garden," Kurt said from behind her, making her jump a little. "Sorry, didn't mean to scare you."

"It's beautiful," Anna told him.

"After she died, Dad took over, bit of a labour of love really. He's out here most days, pottering round."

"How long ago did she die?"

"Twenty-four years now. I was a teenager."

"Oh that must have been rough, for all of you."

"Yeah. Anyway, we'd better go." He gave her an apologetic smile. "I need to get to work."

"Oh sorry, yeah, me too." Anna followed him inside. Kurt gave her a curious look.

"What do you do for work?"

"Oh, I'm just helping Mary in the cafe," Anna told him. "Just this week probably, while the van gets fixed. She's hurt her back." He had a strange look on his face, like he was studying her and she felt a bit flustered. "I'm not a plumber, I can't even change a washer. I flooded the tyre shop trying to ..." she trailed off when he started to laugh. It was a nice laugh, she thought, nothing like Greg's booming guffaw. They looked at each other for a beat, that weird sort of frisson between them, and then a truck rattled past and the moment was gone.

◇

The garage was quiet when Kurt pulled up. A pigeon cooed softly in the stillness and someone slammed a door. The stretch of grass at the kerb was frosty. A tween-aged boy slunk along the footpath, head down, newspaper bag weighing down one shoulder. He gave Kurt an eyebrow raise and a grunt in reply to his greeting.

"Why don't you put your stuff in the back of my car for now," Kurt suggested. "I can take it home after my shift. Do you mind if I have a quick look in the van? See if I can find anything?"

"Okay, yeah, sure. Just give me a minute to change," Anna agreed, and made a quick visit to the bathroom, toothbrush in hand. The shower looked like it had never been used, or cleaned. Cobwebs hung across the sliding door and something musty grew by the drain. Anna was glad she didn't have to use it after all. She had to resort to the supermarket undies, and wondered vaguely if Kurt would be okay with her using his machine to do a wash. She was ready in five minutes and she laughed to herself at how long it normally took her, with all her skincare routines and makeup. It was nice not to feel like she had to put on a face for a change.

When she came out, Kurt was looking under the seats with a penlight, and Anna spent far too long looking at his arse before she gathered up her things from the back.

"Nothing unusual that I can see," Kurt declared, and then looked at her overnight bag. "Is that all you've got?" He looked incredulous.

"Well, I didn't plan to be away long," Anna said. "I'll tell you about it tonight?" That felt weird, she thought, like they were a couple or something. "Anyway, I'd better get going."

"Okay, do you need me to pick you up?" He sounded awkward too, she thought.

"No, no, I can walk."

He fiddled with his keyring and took off a key. "For the back door," he told her. "I won't be back till about six. I have training."

Anna took the key and slid it onto the casino keyring along with Rizzo's.

"Right, thanks. Umm, shall I cook dinner?" God, it was like they were newly married, she thought, all nervous and excited.

"Oh well, sure, if you want? I mean, I can pick up take-aways ..."

"No, no, I'd like to, really. To thank you for letting me stay."

"Sure, okay, thanks. Let me give you my number in case ..."

"Right, yes." Anna took out her phone, and they exchanged information. He picked up her bag and they stood awkwardly.

"Okay, so, see you later then?" Anna said, and then scuttled off down the street, giving him a weird little wave like the Queen.

◇

She spent the morning making scones and muffins and overthinking what she should make Kurt for dinner.

"Darling," Mary asked as they set up the counter food,

"where are you staying? At Paradise? Because I have a spare room if you need it. It's a bit poky, but you're welcome to it if need be."

"Oh, thanks, Mary, but I'm actually at Kurt and his dad's."

"Oh, he didn't say. Oh, well, that's wonderful. So much nicer than a hotel. Not that Bev isn't lovely, but it's so much nicer to be in a real house, isn't it?"

Anna thought of all the five-star hotels she'd been in, and of the lumpy bed in Rizzo, and then of the feeling of being at Kurt's and had to agree.

◇

At about ten she got a call from Faith so she made a coffee and took a break to chat to her.

"I just got a call from Cliff," Faith told her. "The part he went to pick up is for a Toyota Hilux, not a Hiace, or something like that."

"Oh shit."

"Yeah, but he's found another part in Christchurch and they're going to courier it to Mike so he can get it in and the van up and going as soon as possible."

"Oh, well, that's good," Anna said, but she felt weirdly disappointed at the thought of leaving. She watched Mary serving a customer and felt bad leaving her to cope alone when she was gone.

"How are things there?" Faith asked, so Anna gave her a rundown on the events of last night.

"Do you think it was that Gary guy?" Faith asked.

"Was that his name? Yeah, I think so. No idea why though." She made a mental note to tell Kurt the name. "Anyway, tell me all about the Palace?"

They talked for a bit about Isaac and Keith. He'd loved the sculpture Red had made and had hung it up immediately. Faith gave her a rundown about her dad and his illness.

"For some stupid reason I'm contemplating going to see him," Faith said. "I must be mad."

"Well, he is still your father," Anna said. "No matter what. Greg hasn't been the best at parenting, and God knows I did the lion's share of the work, but the kids still love him, and that's how it should be. You don't want to have regrets."

"Hmm, maybe. Anyway, sorry, but I have to run. I'm catching up with an old school friend."

"All right, talk soon." Anna ended the call and sat finishing her coffee, which had gone a bit cold. Mary was chatting with a customer and the sun was shining onto the glass cabinet. I could get used to this life, Anna thought. Simple. Real. The oven timer beeped and she got up to retrieve the quiches out of the oven with a smile.

◇

That afternoon, after picking up some groceries, Anna walked back to Kurt's and through the backyard to the back door. The garden was in full sun so she put the food away and then took a glass of water and sat out on the deck for a bit. She would need to get some more shoes, she thought. All she'd packed were a pair of heels and her boots and her feet were sore. She had so many pairs of shoes at home it was a bit embarrassing, but all she really missed were her Allbirds.

The herb garden smelt amazing. The basil was going mad and the bees were loving the tops that had started to flower. She'd decided to do a lamb rack so she was glad to see there was a heap of rosemary too.

It was peaceful here, and she hadn't had a lot of time lately to just sit and think. She was going to have to get on to a lawyer. One of her Zumba friends had gone through a messy divorce a year or so back, so she sent her a quick message asking who she'd used. What else? She really needed to talk to the kids. But she wanted to make a plan.

What would she do for work? She couldn't stand the thought of going back to office work. She was really enjoying being back in a commercial kitchen, but her CV wouldn't have any recent experience and the money she would make as a low-level kitchenhand would never cover living in a city like Auckland.

There would be enough eventually to buy a house but did she want to go back to Auckland? She had a few friends there, but no one she was super-close to. And none of the kids would be there. Should she move closer to them? She contemplated moving back with her parents for all of about three seconds. Maybe Raglan, to be near Josh? A small town would be nice for a change of pace. A place like Bode where everyone knew you and no one cared what you drove.

Could she stay here? She could keep working for Mary, rent a room maybe until she sorted out things with Greg money-wise. Would that be crazy? One of the swallows landed on the chair opposite and sat looking at her, its head tilted in a quizzical expression. It chirped loudly. "I wish I knew," Anna told it before she got up to sort out some washing.

◇

After she'd prepped Hasselback potatoes and made a glaze for the baby carrots, Anna decided to have a quick vacuum and a clean of the bathroom. Kurt and his dad were pretty tidy, but she wanted to do her bit to thank Kurt for letting her stay. She set the table and prepped the lamb and forced herself not to go into Kurt's room and smell his sheets or anything weird like. It did occur to her that if she stayed in Bode, she might be able to ask him out. Bloody hell, just the thought made her squirm. Did people even date any more? She so did not want to have to use any online dating apps.

It was after six so she opened the bottle of Pinot Noir she'd picked up and poured a glass. Then she sat on the couch and sent off a few texts to the kids and to Faith.

"Bloody hell, it smells fantastic in here," Kurt said as he came through the door. Anna got up and waggled the wine bottle at him in a silent question. "Yeah, that looks good, thanks." She poured him a glass and topped up her own. Kurt had showered and the ends of his hair were still damp against his collar. He smelt faintly of liniment.

"How was your day?" he asked. "Any sign of that Mazda or the guy in it?"

"Faith tells me he said his name was Gary," she told him, "but no, no sign of him. Hopefully he's given up after being chased by you."

"Hmmm, maybe. I've sent out a request for info on the plates in any case. Might hear back tomorrow depending how busy they are."

"I hope you don't mind but I used your washing machine. I was getting dangerously low on clothes."

"Ah, that explains why you're back in my sweats," he said.

"Yeah, it was that or the *Baywatch* T-shirt. Although I noticed you used to be a fan." Kurt did a weird cough and took a large gulp of his wine. Was he blushing? God, he was cute.

"The poster, I mean," Anna clarified. "In what I'm guessing was your room?"

"My room, yeah, right." His eyes had moved to her chest and he looked up at her a little guiltily.

The oven timer dinged and Anna pulled out the lamb to rest for a bit while she glazed the carrots.

"I hope your dad won't mind that I raided his garden?" she said, adding some thyme to the pan.

"No, he'd love it. He's forever giving things away to the neighbours and to Mike and Wayne."

They sat and ate, with Kurt complimenting everything and having seconds.

"This is bloody good. I haven't had such a good meal since my mum was around."

"Did your wife not cook then?" Anna asked. Kurt's eyebrow raised and Anna flushed. "Gina might have mentioned you were divorced," she said.

"Did she now?" Kurt said with a little grin. "Yeah, high school sweethearts. Didn't work out. We've stayed friends though. Her new husband is a good mate actually. They live just out of Balclutha. But no, she wasn't much of a cook – don't tell her I said that though." Anna laughed. "So, how about you? You said 'ex-husband' yesterday?"

"Oh, yes. Well, very recently separated. But a long time coming, you know? He's not taking it well, but it's very definitely over. We hadn't been happy for years. I stayed far too long for the kids' sake, which was a bit silly really." She was rambling. "Do you have any? Kids?"

"No, Jules wasn't keen, and I didn't really care either way to be honest. How many do you have?"

"Three. Two boys and a girl. The older two are twins." She told him a bit about them and that led to how she and Faith had met, and the events leading up to them landing in Bode. By the time she got to the drama at the bank he was roaring with laughter. She really did like his laugh.

They did the dishes together, her loading the dishwasher while Kurt scrubbed the baking dish.

"I made custard tarts at Mary's today, so if you're still hungry, there's a few in the fridge."

"Maybe later," he said. "I'm stuffed." There was a bit of an awkward pause. It was still only eight o'clock and a bit early to go to bed.

"I guess I'll go fold the ..."

"Would you like to watch ..."

They both spoke at once, then laughed.

"I was going to ask if you wanted to watch a movie?" Kurt said.

"Oh, well, okay, yeah, that sounds good."

They went into the lounge and sat on separate couches. Kurt fiddled around with the remotes and brought up Netflix.

"Any requests?" he asked.

"Oh, how about *Baywatch*?" Anna said, just to see him blush again.

They chose *The Inception* with Benedict Cumberbatch and Anna leant back to get comfy, resting her head against the back of the couch where a crochet rug was draped. It was lovely and soft and she pulled it down over her lap.

"This is gorgeous," she said, admiring the blue and green pattern. "Where did you get it?"

Kurt looked a little awkward. "Did your mum make it?" she asked carefully.

"No, actually, I did."

Anna looked at his face to see if he was kidding, but he looked sheepish, a bit embarrassed.

"Really?"

"Yeah, my nana taught me when I was a kid and I just do

it sometimes when I'm bored. Stuck in the car or at night, you know? To kill time." He sounded a bit defensive. Anna guessed it wasn't the usual hobby for such a – manly – sort of guy.

"So how many have you made?" she asked.

"I dunno, a couple of dozen maybe?"

Anna cast a furtive glance around the room looking to see if she had missed a large pile of crochet blankets somewhere.

"Where are they all?"

"Some I've given to people when they have kids, but I usually take them down to the retirement village and give them to the oldies." He looked firmly at the TV as he spoke. "They get cold knees," he added a bit grumpily, as if she was about to argue with him. Anna watched him, resolutely watching the movie.

"Well, I think that's lovely," she said quietly. "You're very talented." He shrugged, looked over at her briefly before standing up.

"I might just have one of those tarts," he said. "Can I get you one? Or tea? Coffee?"

She wanted to tell him not to be embarrassed, but instead she just nodded.

"Tea would be perfect, thanks."

Chapter nineteen

Bode Chronicle:

BRIDGE VS DUNNY BOGS UP TRAFFIC IN BODE

Repairs will need to be made to the Bode bridge after an incident this morning involving a plumber's van, a decorative toilet and a misjudgment by local towie Mike Baker.

The mechanic was left feeling a little flushed today after he drove a van under the bridge without first assessing the load on top, which plunged straight into the bridge.

The bright-pink plumber's van was momentarily stuck, causing the morning traffic to bank up, until the loo was levelled. Minor cosmetic damage to the bridge will be repaired as soon as possible and there was no structural risk found.

Mike came in the next morning looking to buy a sausage roll.

He was looking rather dishevelled, his grey Henley sporting a large patch of baby vomit on the left shoulder, and his hair sticking up on one side. The baby was teething, he told Mary, who was most sympathetic.

"Of course in my day, we'd have rubbed whisky on their gums. They don't do that now, I don't think?"

"No, but I might try it myself tonight," he said with a wink.

He told Anna that the part had arrived on the courier and he needed the keys to start working on the van. He hoped to have it running again early that afternoon. She asked him if he could check out her spare tyre too, in case the patch wasn't up to much and he said it wouldn't be a problem.

As she beat the batter for chocolate cake, Anna contemplated having to leave in a couple of days, once Faith got back. The thought didn't feel great.

She and Mary had a busy morning and she felt like she was getting the hang of Mary's system. She stayed mainly in the back, prepping and baking while Mary served and chatted to customers. She seemed to know them all, and well. From who they were romantically involved with to all their health complaints, as well as who had a beef with whom. Gina had nothing on Mary, Anna decided.

She and Mary talked about their lives. She told the older lady about her childhood, her kids, and her decision to end her marriage. Mary was a good listener, and only offered advice when asked, Anna realised.

"What about you ?" Anna asked. "How did you become the

owner of all this?"

"Oh, it was my Stanley's family business," Mary said. "His father started it as a tea room years ago, back when there was more industry here. The freezing works and such. I wanted to be a nurse. The hospital in 'Clutha had free housing and I thought it would be a great way to get out of home." Anna gave her a sad look. "Oh, it wasn't that I had an awful childhood. I just had four brothers. I wanted some space!" She laughed. "But then I met Stanley, and he swept me off my feet." She looked a little wistful. "We had some happy years here. We worked well together." She smiled at Anna. "A bit like you and me. An easy rhythm. He was always the better baker too, he taught me how to get those scones just right." She passed Anna a block of butter from the fridge and began laying bread out for more club sandwiches. "After he died, I just kept the shop going, I suppose. I'd given up on the idea of nursing by then."

"And no kids?" Anna asked carefully.

"No. Stan had mumps as a kid. Couldn't have them. I have lots of nieces and nephews, but kids weren't on the cards for us. And to be honest, I didn't mind. Stan and I had each other."

"It sounds like you're close with your family," Anna commented. "Do none of them want to be part of Duncan's Doughnuts?"

Mary laughed. "No, they're all terrible in the kitchen. My mother was an old-fashioned woman. She taught me all her cooking skills, but not my brothers. And they all married what I call 'microwave wives' – you know, those women who defrost the meat and cook the outer edge grey at the same time? And make nachos by putting pre-grated cheese on a bag of Doritos."

Anna laughed. "That sounds like my brother's ex. She could overcook water."

"Here, let's finish these and have a cuppa, shall we?" Mary said, mashing up the eggs. "I'm dying for one. And now I have a hankering for a scone."

◇

"I'll see you in the morning then," Anna said to Mary as they locked up that afternoon.

"Oh no, dear, I don't open Saturdays any more. Too old for that lark. I'll be watching my nephew play rugby in the afternoon." She put the key into the pocket of her coat. "Actually, if you'd like to, why don't you come down and watch the game – keep me company? I'll bring a thermos of coffee."

Why not? Anna thought. She'd used to enjoy going to Cameron's games when he'd played and the thought of watching a bunch of grown men running around a field in fitted shorts wasn't unappealing.

◇

There was no sign of Mike when she arrived at the garage, or of Rizzo either. For a moment Anna stood puzzled until she heard and then a second later saw the bright-pink van coming up the road towards her. There was something different though and at first she couldn't put her finger on it. Mike jumped out of the driver's seat and looked sheepish when he saw her.

"Ah shit, Anna — isn't it? Sorry, mate, I had a bit of a run-in with a low-lying bridge."

She noticed then what was different about the van. All that was left of the toilet was a lump of cement and a few remaining pieces of jagged ceramic.

"Oh. Well, you know we're not really plumbers, right? You just did us a favour actually."

"For real? Shit, that's a relief then. Thought your van was a bit crap, to be honest."

Anna didn't think the pun was intended. Mike's eyes widened suddenly. "Fuck, are you, like, fugitives or something? Is the van stolen?"

"No, it's a long story though. So, is she running okay then?"

"Yeah, yeah, she's all good. I'll fix the timing and give her an oil change and she'll be good to go. I'm going to put her inside. Had a call from Kurt just before and he doesn't want her sitting out in the yard overnight. Are you sure you're not, like, running from the law or something?"

"Mike, Kurt is the law."

"Oh yeah, true." He grinned at his stupidity. "Better get on with it, I guess. Got Audrey Graham's car in for a warrant while my wife is doing her pedi and she'll be spewing if it's not finished when she's done."

Anna tried hard not to think about Audrey's toes.

◇

Kurt was mowing the lawns and Anna stood on the back deck surveying the garden. It was a garden her father would be proud of — neat rows of spinach and broccoli, the crimson tops of beetroot peeking out of the soil below their lush green leaves. Cursing her lack of sensible shoes, Anna pulled off her boots and winced her way over the crushed shell path in her bare feet. She'd heaped a decent pile of weeds to the side of the garden when she heard a sound and looked up.

"You've been working hard. You didn't need to though. Don't want you to feel you have to work to pay for your board, Anna."

Kurt stood watching her, sweating lightly. She'd been so engrossed she hadn't heard him turn off the mower and had no idea how long he'd been standing there for.

"I don't mind. Quite enjoy it actually. We had a decent vege garden when I was growing up."

"Here, at least put some gumboots on. They're Dad's so they're probably a bit big." He jogged over to her, a pair of Red Bands in his hand. They were indeed too big but Anna put them on gratefully. Her toes were pink from the cold and covered in dirt.

"Thanks." She straightened up again. They were standing

less than a metre apart. So close she could see the faint imprint of frown lines on his forehead and the crinkles around his eyes. There was only a couple of inches difference in their height and they were almost at eye level. He lifted the hem of his shirt to wipe his face and Anna could see his stomach, all the ridges and grooves and a happy trail ... and oh, my God, look up, Anna! she told herself. But when she did he was leaning into her, his hand up by her cheek and holy hell! Was he going to ...? She closed her eyes.

"Ladybug," he said, pulling something from her hair. She sighed a little. In regret, not relief.

"Oh. Well. I'm not scared of bugs," she said stupidly. She couldn't believe she'd thought he was going to kiss her. Kurt cleared his throat and they both turned back to the garden. She attacked the weeds, willing her red cheeks to go away.

"So where was home? As a child?"

"I grew up on a farm in the Waikato. My parents are still there and my older brother runs it now. It hasn't been all designer clothes and fancy city lifestyle for me."

"I never said it was. Never thought that at all."

Anna looked down at her mud-smeared jeans. "No, I know. But that's what I was like for a long time."

Kurt didn't know that Anna. Since he'd met her she'd been the new Anna and she was glad about that. The old Anna could be impatient, tooting at cars that weren't going fast enough — God forbid she arrive five minutes late for her yoga class — and way more serious than this Anna. There hadn't been much to smile about in the last few years. Since she'd been on this trip with Faith, she'd been way more relaxed and had more fun than she could remember having in a long time.

Working with her hands again gave her purpose and it felt good to be helping Mary out. She'd used to volunteer at the SPCA when she was a student and had forgotten how good it felt to do something for someone else. She felt suddenly ashamed she'd been so selfish for so long, not thinking of anyone much beyond her own family.

"Come on, let's get cleaned up," Kurt said standing and stretching. "I'm taking you for dinner at the RSA to say thank you for all your hard work. It won't be as good as our meal last night but they do a pretty good fish and chip Friday."

The RSA consisted of a paisley-carpeted seating area with Formica tables with vinyl chairs and a wood-floored bar area with an old snooker table and half a dozen bar leaners. It smelt faintly of fried food and it was a little rundown, but clean and inviting with a low hum of voices.

It seemed like half the town was at the RSA for Friday night and Anna said as much to Kurt as they waited at the bar for drinks.

"Yeah, and the other half are at O'Leary's," he laughed. "But no, actually, Bode's got a good mix really. Older people, young families. We're big enough to have a high school — just. It's a good community and pretty supportive. If anyone needs something, there'll be a fundraiser and we all chip in."

"So how many police officers then? Is it just you?"

"No, my partner Wayne too. We cover a decent area, including the smaller towns that don't have their own station. We have the wonderful Kath who does all our office work but only two holding cells. Only time it ever got crowded was when Mike and Tina's wedding got out of hand and we had to throw three of my cousins in there to sober up for the night."

"Oh shit, that doesn't sound too good."

"Nah, it was a great night. Except that Mike was one of the guys in the lockup and Tina was pretty pissed off with him." He grinned and Anna laughed.

They carried their drinks and a laminated menu over to a small square table and sat down.

"So what made you decide to be a cop?" Anna asked, sipping her wine. Kurt gave her a contemplative look.

"I was a bit of a wayward teen," he told her. "After Mum died, I went off the rails a bit, I suppose. No direction, small town, so all the usual bullshit. Underage drinking, smoked a bit of the 'green friend' you mentioned, a bit of vandalism, tagging and the like."

Anna was surprised. It was hard to imagine.

"It must have been hard losing her when you did," she said. "Do you have any siblings?"

"Yeah, an older brother. He was at uni when she got sick. Lives in Dunedin now with his own family."

"And how did your dad take it?"

"Oh, he was a wreck. Which was why he didn't notice I was

being a little shit. I got caught eventually though. The local cop, Les Borich, caught me smashing a window at the high school." He paused to take a drink. "Anyway, he sat me down and gave me a bit of a talking to. And something he said must have just clicked, I guess. He let me off, made me repair the window, told Dad he needed to keep an eye on me more. It worked for both of us, snapped us out of things."

"And so you joined the force?"

"Yeah, I think I just realised that it was a good place to help people who needed it, you know? That if Les could make a difference for me, I might be able to do the same." He looked a little shy as he said it. "So off I went to training, and off to Dunedin for a bit, then Les retired, and the job came up here."

"I bet Cliff was happy you came back."

"Yeah, I guess. He and I get along pretty well. I only moved in with him a few years ago though. I thought he could do with the help." He shrugged. "And I wanted to get a dog," he added with a grin. "It's a big place for just him, but he wouldn't sell it. He's getting on now, but he's a stubborn bugger and he won't retire yet either."

"Did he want you to take over at the garage?"

"Nah, not particularly. And Mike's been hanging round there since he could hold a spanner. Every day after school since he was a teenager, and Dad finally took him on."

He picked up the menu and Anna suspected he was uncomfortable talking so much about himself. She picked her own menu up.

"So, fish and chips, you say?"

◇

While Kurt went to place their order, Anna got up to use the bathroom. It was very outdated, but spotlessly clean and the stalls were empty. She was coming out of one when the door opened behind her and she found herself being thrust hard up against the wall next to the hand-dryer.

"Where's the fucking van?"

A sweaty hand pressed firmly against her throat and she choked slightly, unable to answer.

"Answer me, bitch. What've you done with the van?"

She vaguely recognised that it was the guy from outside the cafe in Dunedin, the one in the red car and possibly the same guy who had almost attacked her in the garage the other night. His eyes were bloodshot and darting about wildly. There was a stale, rancid odour to him. He didn't seem steady on his feet and she wondered whether he was drunk, or maybe high. His hand loosened slightly.

"I haven't done anything with it, it's getting fixed," she gasped.

"I need something I left in it." He swayed and removed his hand from around her neck but was still pinning her against the wall by her shoulders.

"There's nothing in it you could want. Your weed's not there, if that's what you're after."

"What weed?" He looked confused. "Nah, bitch, I left something else in there eh?" He leaned so close she could smell his fetid breath. "You fucking take me there right now. I've got debts, man. I need it, okay?"

"What do you need? There's nothing in there," Anna repeated.

"I'm in the shit okay? *Fuck!*" He let go of her and violently punched the wall. Anna seized the opportunity. She shoved him with both hands and he stumbled back and then slipped, sprawling onto the floor. She spun and yanked the door open, ran down the hall, too terrified to look back to see if he was following her.

When Anna arrived back in the dining room, everything seemed just as she'd left it. Around half the patrons looked up at her appearance though, gasping and dishevelled in the doorway, including Kurt. He took one look at her and stood and they met in the middle of the room.

"What's going on? Are you okay, what happened?"

"Gary," she gasped. "He just attacked me in the bathroom."

Without a word he was off and Anna was left staring after him. She'd started to shake and felt like she might pass out. Never in her life had she been the subject of violence, apart from a bit of roughhousing with her brothers, and now twice in one week she'd almost been attacked. She felt a gentle hand on her elbow and someone led her over to a chair. A glass of amber-coloured liquid was pushed into her hand — brandy, she realised, spluttering as she took a large gulp. She tossed the rest of it back gratefully.

Kurt came back while she was sipping at a second glass, looking grim.

“No sign of him, he probably went out a side door. I’ve called it in to Wayne and he’s going to have a look around. I should go help him.” He reached for his jacket, looking uncertain.

“No, stay here with me.” The thought of him leaving made Anna feel panicky. “It’s your night off, have something to eat. Please.” Her voice was shaky.

Kurt looked down at her. He reached out and gently touched her neck where she could feel the marks Gary had left.

“All right,” he said. “You want another drink?”

“Could you get me a wine? Anything red will be fine.”

◇

“So, what exactly did he say to you?” Kurt asked when he came back, carrying a bottle and two glasses. Anna told him what had happened.

“He seemed desperate. For some reason he thinks there’s something in there and he really wants it back. Not the drugs. I wonder if his mate Baz took whatever it is out before he sold us the van?”

“Yeah, possibly. I had a feeling he might come back. That’s why I asked Mike to put the van inside the shed. We’ve had a few reports of petty theft — little stuff like a sleeping bag and food. Someone had some clothes stolen off their clothesline."

"You think it might be Gary?"

"Wayne was called out this morning because a guy thought someone had been sleeping out in his shed. It might be nothing but it is unusual behaviour for around here. I'd like to get hold of him and have a talk to him, and he's assaulted you now as well, not just threatened to."

Wayne called when they'd just finished their food to say there was no sign of Gary, or of the red Mazda they suspected he was driving, but he'd go back out for another look later. He was going to keep an eye on the garage as well. The info on the plates hadn't come back yet and Kurt was hoping to hear the next day.

"I'll get us a nightcap," Anna said, when Kurt told her all this. Kurt didn't object and she saw again the merits of living in a small town where almost everything was within walking distance and you could have a few drinks.

She'd had far more of the wine than Kurt and was feeling pleasantly buzzed when they got up to leave. In fact, more than pleasantly buzzed she realised as she tripped over a plastic mat at the bottom of the stairs and felt her ankle twist. Anna tumbled into Kurt, clutching at his arm to hold herself up, but still managed to slide down onto the floor in a most ungainly manner.

"Whoops, *ow*."

"Are you okay?"

Kurt reached down and grabbed her hand to pull her up, but when she tried to stand she realised she couldn't put any weight on her foot.

"No, I think I've sprained my bloody ankle." She took a hobbling step, but pain shot up her leg. "Oh shit, you're going to have to piggyback me home," she giggled.

Kurt regarded her for a moment. "I can do one better than that." He scooped her up into his arms and pushed the door to the RSA open with his hip, easing them through.

"I was just joking. You can't lug me all the way back. I'm way too heavy."

"Hardly," he huffed, walking along the quiet street with long strides.

"At least you're not carrying me fireman-style, I guess. Because you're a policeman, aren't you?" Was she slurring?

"I am indeed," Kurt replied, sounding amused as he crossed over the road, nodding casually at someone walking towards them.

"Your police uniform is much sexier than a fireman's uniform. Fireman pants are way too baggy."

He laughed, his chest rumbling where Anna leaned her head, feeling lulled by the movement of his body. "So strong," she mumbled.

She may have dozed off, because then he was fumbling by her butt, reaching for the lock on his door and then they were inside.

"You know, if this was a movie, you'd be kissing me right

now," she said.

He was watching her intently, his eyes hooded and he leant in, their lips so close she could feel his breath. Her heart pounded. She wanted to kiss him so badly, and then he was pulling away, setting her down gently in the hallway.

"I'll get you some Panadol," he said. "And some water."

He thought she was drunk. Maybe she was. Her ankle had started to ache and she went into her room, shut the door carefully and stood, feeling like an idiot. She heard him coming back down the hall.

"Anna?" he called softly, but she couldn't bring herself to answer. After a beat, he left, and she heard his door open, and then close. She hobbled over to the bed, carefully pulled off her boots, wincing at her swollen ankle, and got in, fully clothed, feeling stupidly close to tears. Her head swam a bit. Eventually, she fell asleep.

Chapter twenty

The next morning she woke early to the sound of the blender going in the kitchen. Pamela Anderson looked down on her from the wall beside her. She lay and listened to Kurt moving around the house, dreading the thought of seeing him. The front door opened, and she heard his car start up and pull away.

Her head and her ankle both throbbed. She pulled the covers back over her head.

Eventually she got up and hobbled to the shower. When she got out she discovered he'd left the Panadol and a glass of water on the bench. She gulped them down and then made herself a coffee and a piece of toast and sat down at the table to eat, resting her ankle on a chair.

She was still sitting there about an hour later, trying to muster some energy and seriously contemplating going back to bed, when there was a quick rap at the door, before it opened.

"Yoo-hoo, only me," Mary called. Shit. She'd forgotten about the rugby. "I heard you hurt your ankle last night, so I've brought some sneakers and a compression sock," she said. "You were the talk of the town again this morning, what with Kurt going all Richard Gere on you, carrying you out of the RSA like a re-enactment of an officer and a gentleman."

Anna groaned.

"Come on then, let's see about that foot and then we'll head off. I've got lunch in the car. You look like you need some fresh air."

They drove a little way out of the town to a large sports field. There was a square, two-storey clubhouse with what looked like locker rooms or toilets on the lower concrete brick level. Floodlights stood at one end, with several marked rugby pitches as well as a cricket cage along one side. Beside the grounds was an asphalt netball court.

The rugby grounds were surprisingly busy and the car park was full when they arrived, but Mary pulled up into the disabled park by the clubhouse and gave Anna a grin.

"The only person in town with a permit is Glenn Fairbanks and he's away in Stewart Island visiting his son. He's promised me some crayfish when he gets back too."

They got out of the car, Anna gingerly testing her foot on the grass, but Mary had done a good job of it and it felt nice and secure. Mary went round to the boot and extracted two camp chairs and gave one to Anna to carry.

A large group of supporters stood along the sideline, chatting and cupping takeaway coffees. Gina was there and gave them a wave, so they set up next to her. She was dressed in a black puffer jacket, jeans and leopard print gumboots and was nursing a keep cup, stamping her feet to keep them warm.

"Hey, how's it going? I heard you had a bit of drama last night. How's the ankle?"

"Man, I'd forgotten how good the grapevine is in small towns," Anna said with a laugh, her breath frosty in the cold air. "It's fine, just a bit of a sprain. Nothing serious. I need to buy some flat shoes though."

"Oh you can keep those ones," Mary said, indicating the sneakers she had loaned her. Gina did a weird cough/laugh and Anna tried not to grin. The shoes were pink and orange orthopedics, with chunky soles. Even Anna's mother would have passed on them. But it was very kind of her.

"Thanks, Mary," she said, taking the offered thermos lid of coffee.

"If it makes you feel better, Mike is the biggest news today, taking the loo off your van like that," Gina said. "That was classic." Anna laughed. A whistle blew and then the two teams were running out onto the field, their breath steaming in the crisp air. There were a lot of tight shorts and muscular thighs going past, a bit of banter and spitting and re-inserting of mouth guards.

"That's Kurt's ex," Gina told her, pointing across the field to a tall dark-haired woman in black sweats and a baggy jumper. She looked up and waved and Gina waved back.

"She and I never used to hang out much at high school but we became mates when Kurt and her started dating. She's nice. You'll like her. They'll probably have a drink in the clubhouse later. That's her hubby there, the bald one with the tape over his ears."

"Which one is your nephew, Mary?" Anna asked, scanning the players.

Kurt was there, she realised, stretching his Achilles and laughing with a familiar-looking guy with a shock of red hair. The guy from the photo, she thought. His partner, Wayne. She should have known he'd play rugby, but for some reason she had imagined he'd gone to work, and she felt flustered to see him there.

"Dion? He's the big one at the back with the white-blond hair," Mary said, but Kurt had looked up and seen her, gave her a smile and she found herself unable to look away. She gave him a self-conscious wave and Gina snorted next to her.

"What?" she said, pulling her scarf up round her chin.

"You've got it bad," Gina laughed.

"Oh, shut up," Anna said, going red. "I just didn't realise Kurt played. I thought he'd left early this morning for work."

"Oh no, dear," Mary said. "He would have been here setting up and reffing and what not. He coaches the littlies, you know. Has done for years. He's wonderful with them."

Anna's heart gave a little lurch and she gave herself a stern talking to as the whistle blew to start the game.

◇

◇

The game was a close one, and Anna found herself cheering along just as loudly as everyone else. Kurt was a good player, and she watched him a lot. When the full-time whistle went and the teams had shaken hands, he came jogging over, all sweaty, his shirt sticking to his chest. Anna made herself look only at his face.

"Hey, I didn't know you'd be here," he said, smiling. "How's the ankle?"

"It's fine. I came to watch Dion," she told him. "It was a good game."

"Right. Yeah. You sticking around for a drink then?" he asked. He wasn't smiling now. He looked a little pissed.

"Yeah, we'll see you in the clubhouse," Gina said, holding out an arm to help Anna out of her chair.

◇

The clubrooms had the same smell of clubrooms everywhere. Stale beer, sweat and Old Spice. Wooden plaques lined the walls, some of them faded with age, others newer, the shiny fresh writing announcing player of the season and tournament wins from as recent as the previous year.

Mary and Anna sat on high stools at one of the old wood benches while Gina went off to get the first round of drinks. People had exchanged coats and umbrellas for pints and toasted sandwiches and there was a constant hum of voices and the odd loud burst of laughter. It reminded Anna of all the times she and her brothers had spent at the clubhouse with her dad, begging for a packet of chips and a lemonade.

Gina came back with all the drinks triangled in her hands and a packet of peanuts between her teeth, which she spat out onto the table.

"They're going to give Mike the Darwin Award later," she laughed. "Very fitting since it's a gold toilet seat."

"His name's on that bloody thing more than anyone's," Mary laughed, opening the nuts.

◇

After a bit the players started to filter in. Mary's nephew Dion was one of the first out and he came over to give Mary a kiss on the cheek.

"Hey, aunty."

"Hello, love, you played well. Did you get a drink? You did? Good, sit and meet Anna then." Dion was tall and lanky with a smattering of freckles across his nose. He was about thirty, she would guess, and his platinum-white hair was spiked up. He gave Anna a wide smile and then a kiss on the cheek too, before sitting next to her, pulling his chair up close.

"All right then?"

"Hi, Dion. Good game."

A few other players came over and talked to Gina and then Kurt was there, scowling at her like she'd done something wrong. Wayne was with him and leant across the table to shake her hand.

"You must be Anna," he said. "Kurt and Gina have told me lots about you. Then he kissed Gina on the top of the head. "Hello, love, do you need a top-up?"

"Wait, Wayne's your husband?" Anna said to Gina, who laughed.

"Yep. This old thing's all mine." She gave Wayne a fond pat on his arse. "I'll have another gin, thanks, babe. Mary? Anna?"

"No, I better be off actually," Mary said. "Dion, will you give Anna a lift home?"

Anna was still trying to process the fact that Wayne and Gina were a couple. Shit. She'd gone on and on to Gina about how hot Kurt was. Would she have told Wayne? Who would then have told Kurt?

"Anna?" Gina was saying.

"Sorry, what?"

"Kurt was saying he'd take you home if that was okay?" Anna looked up at Kurt, freshly showered and still scowling.

"I just said it was stupid for Dion to, since you're at my house," he muttered. Anna couldn't read his tone.

"Oh right, yes, thanks."

"So another drink then?" Wayne asked.

"Actually, I might just have an orange juice. Kurt, if you want to drink, I'm happy to drive if you're okay with that?" He gave her a long look that made Anna nervous. "I mean, I had a bit much last night, so I'm happy to let you drink if you want? I don't drink that much anyway normally and ..." she trailed off when he smiled.

"Yeah, that would be great, are you sure?"

Wayne gave a whoop. "Alrighty then, let's get some beers for the boys." Gina gave Anna an eye-roll. "And a gin for my love," he added.

"I'll go," Kurt offered.

"Sweet. Lager for me, cheers," said Dion, and Kurt glared at him. "Get your own," he told him as he left. Gina laughed.

"Bloody hell, I don't think I've seen Kurt get jealous before," she said.

"Neither have I," someone said behind Anna and when she turned, there was Kurt's ex-wife, grinning at her. "I'm Jules," she said, "and I'm intrigued. Who are you?"

◇

They all shuffled round to make more room and Jules' husband, Dean, pulled up some bar stools. He and Wayne started to chat. Mary did the introductions.

"Jules, this is Anna, she turned up in town in a broken pink van and saved my bacon," she said, patting Anna on the shoulder as she stood to go. "I'll see you Monday, Anna?"

Anna nodded. "Thanks again for the shoes," she said.

After Mary had left, Jules turned her attention to Anna.

"So, the rumour mill tells me you're a plumber?"

Anna laughed and gave her a condensed story of her and Faith's trip. "... And so Kurt was nice enough to offer me a bed," she finished.

"And he's not bad in it either, is he?" Jules said in a stage whisper. "I remember that."

Anna choked on a peanut and Gina gave her a hearty slap on the back as she laughed.

"Oh, I mean it's not, we haven't ..." Anna trailed off and took a sip of her drink, blushing like a teengaer.

"Well, I hope you do," Jules said with a fond smile. "He really is a lovely guy and it would be nice to see him with someone good. The last girl he dated was awful."

"Who dated?" Kurt asked, arriving back at the table with a tray of drinks.

"You," Jules told him. "That Lisa. She was a right cow."

Kurt laughed. "Well, they can't all be perfect like you, Jules."

She gave him the finger with a grin. "How's Cliff?" she asked.

"Good. He's off seeing Des at the moment. He's not doing so good."

"Aww, poor bugger. Tell your dad I said hi, yeah?"

◇

Jules was lovely, Anna decided. She and Dean stayed for a bit to chat but left early. There was no tension at all between her and Kurt, and Anna wondered if she and Greg would ever get to the stage where they could be that friendly. It seemed unlikely.

Kurt and Wayne drank a few pints and Gina had a few more gins. They were joined by some of the other team members, and Jason shouted a round of whiskies. Anna was having a great time chatting and laughing. She kept sneaking looks at Kurt, who caught her several times and gave her a grin. After a bit, she suggested to Gina that she join her in the ladies where she quickly cornered her.

"Please tell me you didn't tell Wayne I was drooling over Kurt?" Gina just laughed. "I can't believe you didn't tell me Wayne was your husband!"

"Babe, it's fine. I'm sure the feeling is mutual. You should totally bust a move."

Anna squirmed. "I did. Last night. He turned me down."

"Really? That's surprising. I mean, look at you, you're gorgeous." Gina did a slightly drunk hand wave to indicate all of Anna's gorgeousness. "Well, maybe he's worried you'll break his heart," she said. "He hasn't dated much since Jules. He's not really a player, you know? And if you're taking off soon …"

"Yeah. I guess. But I don't think I want to. Take off. Not just because of Kurt. But I like it here, I dunno. Maybe I'm being nuts."

"Oh, my God, I would love it if you stayed," Gina squealed excitedly, jumping up and down with her hands on Anna's shoulders. "I feel like we connected, you know? Maybe I'm just drunk, but I feel like we could be besties."

Anna laughed. "Yeah, I know. And I'm not even drunk."

"Stay," Gina said. "Stay and shag Kurt and get drunk with me after rugby games."

They wandered back to the table where Mike had joined them, golden toilet seat around his neck, having a sculling competition with Dion. Kurt looked over at her, mouthed 'You okay?' and she smiled, gave him a thumbs up. She was very okay, she realised. Tomorrow she'd start sorting things. Start planning for a new life.

◇

She drove them home at about ten. They'd had some food at the clubrooms and Kurt was chatty, but not super-drunk. He thanked her again as she pulled up at the house.

"My pleasure," she said, "it was the least I could do after last night."

Kurt opened the front door and gestured her in.

"Anna, about last night. I'm sorry if you thought I was …" He trailed off. She looked up at him and he was looking at her, at her lips and then he lent in, and he kissed her. Softly. Tentatively. He tasted faintly of whisky and she kissed him back, going up on her toes and then pulling back when she remembered her sore ankle.

"Shit, I'm sorry," he said. "I don't know why I did that. I told myself not to rush you. I know you're fresh out of a marriage and it's too soon, and … sorry." He turned and went down the hallway, into his room. Anna stood in the front entrance, her heart beating madly against her ribcage. Should she follow him? *Was* it too soon?

She hobbled down the hallway, got into her pyjamas, brushed her teeth, and lay on Kurt's single bed. She imagined him in his room, lying there thinking of her. It didn't feel too soon to her. She and Greg hadn't been together for years. And emotionally she had left the marriage a long time ago. But Kurt didn't know that. She would have to make the first move. Tomorrow, she resolved.

Chapter twenty-one

However, in the morning, despite her resolutions, Anna was at a bit of a loose end. It was Sunday, so there was no way to talk to the lawyer her friend had put her on to. She left a message on her answer machine. She wanted to talk to Mary, she decided, to see if there was a chance she would eventually sell the business to her, but for now, she just wanted to see if she could stay on as an employee.

Kurt was up before her and went for a run. Anna decided to test her ankle and try a bit of yoga out on the lawn, which was where he found her when he came back. She looked up and found him watching her from the open kitchen window as he drank a glass of water, his Adam's apple bobbing. She gave him a wave.

"Morning. Sorry I'm in your sweats again. But I only have jeans and they just don't work for doing downward dog." He came out onto the deck, two glasses in hand.

"I don't mind. You look better in them than me. But you know, if you needed to get anything, there's a shopping centre in Balclutha. I could take you if you wanted?" He looked a bit awkward so she gave him a smile.

"That would be fantastic. I'll go back to Auckland at some point and pack up all my stuff, but I really am struggling with what I've got on me." She hoped that was hint enough that she planned to stay. She decided to lay her cards on the table a bit more. "Do they have a picture theatre? Maybe I could shout you to the movies?" She was next to him now and she took a glass from his hand, fingers brushing. She took a sip.

"Yeah, yeah, we could do that," he said. They stood drinking water and looking at each other, both grinning.

"I'd better jump in the shower then," he said and Anna briefly contemplated asking if he'd like some company.

◇

"So, Jules seems lovely," Anna said as she put on her seat belt. Kurt smiled.

"Yeah, she's a good sort. So is Dean."

"What does he do?" Anna asked.

"They own a security company," he told her. "I got him to bring me some surveillance stuff for the garage actually."

"It's nice that you're so friendly," Anna said, hoping it didn't sound like she was digging for gossip, which she totally was. Luckily he took the bait.

"Yeah, we had a really easy divorce, all things considered.

Jules has family here, and she had been happy to come home from Dunedin initially, but she got bored. Frustrated really. I was working too much – it was just me back then – and we just got to the stage where we weren't really happy any more, you know?" He gave her a sideways glance and she nodded. "I guess not having kids made the decision easier to move on."

Anna thought about that. About telling the kids she and Greg were done. She'd known they were all old enough to understand, but she had still dreaded it. She had stuck it out for them, thinking that having their parents together was important, but now she realised it was better that they saw her happy. Maybe she and Greg would even get on better once they had both moved on.

She imagined Greg dating again, prodded at the idea like a sore tooth to see if it would hurt. It didn't. But she imagined he'd probably be a cliché and find some younger model to stroke his ego.

"So, what was so awful about Lisa?" she asked. Kurt laughed.

"Nothing really. She was just a bit high maintenance, and hard work." He gave Anna a serious look. "And she wasn't keen on rugby – or dogs," he added.

◇

Balclutha was a slightly bigger town with a long, impressive multi-arched bridge that crossed a heavily swollen river. It had a surprisingly good range of shops and Anna managed to get some clothes for the bakery as well as workout gear and more underwear. She was low on cash so she decided to leave buying shoes and just wear Mary's.

She wondered if Cliff would let her pay off the van repairs. She would need to sell or give it to Faith if she wasn't going to travel back in it straight away. Would she keep her Range Rover? Or sell it and buy something down here?

She stocked up on a few toiletries as well and then she and Kurt had lunch. The cafe wasn't overly busy and they found a small table easily in a corner. The menu was fairly basic. Anna decided on a roast vege salad and a smoothie. Her ankle was a little sore so she fished out some painkillers from her handbag.

Kurt offered to order for them and when he came back to the table, pulled up an extra chair before gently lifting her foot up onto it. His palm felt scorching hot against her ankle and Anna took a long drink of water before she looked up at him. He was watching her intently. That electric energy was back, fizzing between them. Kurt cleared his throat, fiddling with their table number.

"Wayne called. The red Mazda was spotted out near the McCarrolls' farm last night, and Mike is going through footage on the new security camera I installed yesterday to see if he's been lurking around," Kurt said.

"And if he has been?"

"Then we might park the van outside tonight if that's

okay with you? And wait."

"Oh, like a stakeout? Can I come? Please? I'll be quiet as a mouse. You won't even know I'm there."

Kurt grinned. "I think you might be a bit of a distraction even if you were silent," he said, and Anna blushed.

◇

The movies were actually set up in the old theatrical society clubrooms, so there was only one choice. It was a horror movie and Anna was a bit of a chicken when it came to things leaping out at her, but Kurt seemed happy with it so they got popcorn and drinks and settled into the old vinyl chairs.

The movie was terrifying. Anna spent the first half covering her eyes, trying not to scream. At some point she realised she had her hand on Kurt's thigh, gripping hard. She loosened her grip, but then decided to leave it there. It was firm and warm and she wanted to inch it up further. After a while though, he jiggled around and then shifted her hand down closer to his knee. But he left his palm on top of hers. It seared heat through her, like tiny sparks. His hand was a lot bigger and he had nice long, tapered fingers and big tidy nails. He even had sexy wrists and veiny forearms and before she knew it, the movie was done and she'd spent half of it getting turned on by his hand.

He held hers all the way back to the car.

The drive back seemed to take forever. Anna felt like a horny teenager, hoping her date would make a move at the end. Just before they hit Bode, Wayne rang. Kurt put him on speaker.

"Hey, mate, just wanted to let you know those plates you ran came back. They belong to a Maureen Harwick in Christchurch. Red Mazda." Kurt looked at her and she shrugged.

"Did you look her up?" Kurt asked.

"Yep. Has a son Gary. She claims he took the car last week and hasn't come back. And get this: he's wanted for questioning by police in Wellington about that pickled hand that went missing from Te Papa."

"Shit. Okay. Let me check in with Mike, see if there was any sign of him last night. You free to do some surveillance tonight?"

"Yep, all good. You said you checked the van out, yeah?"

"Yeah, but maybe go in and look underneath it."

Kurt hung up and looked at Anna who looked horrified. "Ewww! Do you mean to tell me there might be some mummified hand in Rizzo?" She shuddered. "It did smell a bit musty. What does a hundred-year-old hand smell like?"

Kurt laughed. "I doubt it's just a hand wrapped in bandages. It's probably in formaldehyde or something."

Anna gave him a scathing look. "Oh, well, now I feel so much better," she said sarcastically. He grinned.

"I doubt it's in there anyway. Like you said, maybe his mate took it?"

◇

Back at Kurt's they discovered Gary had been lurking around the garage the night before, the distinctive red Mazda showing up clearly on the video footage.

"Looks like I'll be doing an all-nighter," Kurt said. "I might try and catch a nap before I go."

Anna watched him walk down the hallway, trying to muster up some courage. Just do it, she told herself. Be brave.

"Would you like some company?" she asked.

He turned, gave her an appraising look, and strode back towards her. His face was hard to read. He stood in front of her, looking intently at her eyes. Her pulse was frantic in her throat.

Then he was kissing her, and shit, her insides were melting. He tasted faintly of butter and his hands came up to cradle her face as he pressed his lips more urgently against hers. She made a soft moaning sound against them and he lifted her up, cupping her arse. She pushed her hands up under his shirt, feeling the taut muscles of his back and she wanted to climb inside him. He carried her back down the hallway and into his room and they were scrambling for each other's clothes and Anna thought she might combust.

"Are you sure?" he asked, and she'd never been more sure of anything in her life.

Chapter twenty-two

Southland Times:

COMMUNITY CULT CRACKING THE CORPORATE?

The Servants of Christ religious community have sparked controversy with the latest decision to modernise their growing egg business.

Managing Director Jebediah Mathews takes responsibility for the decision to no longer hand weigh and grade their free-range eggs and instead use industrial machinery – a move he says was necessary in order to comply with the New Zealand egg standards and grades set by the Egg Producers Federation of New Zealand Code of Practice 2002.

The move goes somewhat against the principles of the community, who fear the impact of modernity and the temptations of technology on their children, church and traditional Christian world.

However, Mr Mathews is quick to point out that

this step into the modern world will not affect the way the community lives in their own homes. "We will still hold to our fundamental beliefs, and that of our Lord when we leave work."

New Zealanders eat around 250 eggs per person per year, and God's Own Eggs supply Invercargill with a large number of those, employing 14 workers and with over 5000 free-range hens.

"Thanks again for letting me tag along," Faith said, smiling over at Tania.

"No problem, it's been really nice catching up after all this time. I mean, it's been lovely keeping in touch over Facebook and seeing your kids and everything but it's not quite like being face to face, is it?"

"Definitely not."

"I see your family sometimes when I'm in town visiting Mum. I don't think they remember me at all."

"They wouldn't acknowledge you if they did. I wasn't meant to have any friends outside the community. I really wish we could have had that kind of friendship where we hung out at each other's house on the weekend and went to the movies and stuff. My girls have that, thank goodness. I'm so glad that they do."

"Yeah, well, you were my only friend really. Nobody wanted to hang out with the nerdy kid whose mother was the principal."

"You weren't nerdy, you were smart. Although it wasn't

such a cool thing in those days, was it? Anyway, I'm sure it was because of me they didn't want to hang out with you." They both laughed comfortably. "I'd love to come and say hello to your mum while I'm in town. She was so wonderful at helping me persuade my parents to let me go nursing."

"You should call round if you get time. She'd love to see you too – often asks about you. Don't take this the wrong way but she was so pleased you never came back. She thought you'd end up being forced to."

"Even if I hadn't gotten pregnant I wouldn't have. I was determined it was my way out."

"Yeah, I remember you always said that. Especially once you met Daniel. So, he's still teaching?"

"Yes, and he still loves it. Honestly, the man has the patience of a saint. He's put up with me all these years."

Tania looked over at her briefly before turning her attention back to the road. "I'd hardly say he's had to 'put up with you'. He always adored you and clearly still does. And why wouldn't he? You're lovely."

"He didn't have much choice, did he? The God Squad girl gets knocked up, expects the boy to marry her ..."

"Faith. It's not like you forced him at gunpoint. You guys would have ended up together anyway."

"I don't know. Maybe he would have chosen someone else." It was something Faith had wondered. She'd felt so naive and inexperienced when she'd met Daniel. Fresh out of the Servants. It had been years before she'd really come to terms with her upbringing, and his patience and support had never wavered, but she wondered if they hadn't had Rachel whether things would have ended differently.

"But he did choose you. He was going out with that girl in the room opposite mine – what was her name?"

"Paula White."

"That's right, Paula. And left her broken-hearted because he was smitten with you."

"Me. The strange, quiet one."

"The lovely, quiet one. With a wicked sense of humour. Stop putting yourself down. You guys have been together all this time. That's gotta mean something."

It did, she supposed. They'd weathered the storm of mortgages and parenthood and things hadn't always been easy financially, especially when Faith had gone back to study, but they'd muddled along together. There wasn't anyone she could imagine doing it with other than Daniel.

"So, how was the official opening and birthday bash last night?" Tania asked, and Faith spent the next while regaling her with all the details of the party. The highlight had been doing karaoke with Tim Shadbolt, although he sang terribly.

◇

Tania dropped her at Charity's house just before noon. They travelled up the long sealed road leading to an imposing stone fence with shingle pillars on each side, guarding the entrance. There was nothing to announce the community and no bolted gate separated them from the rest of the town but they were situated slightly into the countryside, a small cluster of streets with modest houses. Her nerves were at their peak by the time they pulled up outside. The house was a wooden, one-level, cottage-style building with plain cotton curtains at the window and a natural timber door.

Faith waved Tania off and stood outside, feeling suddenly nervous. She'd spoken to Charity maybe once a year since she'd left, a bit more recently, but she didn't really know her sister any more. They'd been so close as kids, but when Faith left, it was expected that Charity wouldn't have any contact with her.

Growing up, Charity had been so calm and accepting. So many times she'd covered for Faith, who'd started to question everything, and stopped her from getting into trouble with their father. She was smart but had no desire to further her education, accepting her lot when Jebediah had been selected as her husband. That was probably the thing that had made Faith decide she would push to further her education, seeing her favourite sister married to a man she didn't love, barely knew really, and had no input in choosing. That and hearing Tania talk about things like the boys and parties of the future, like they were the most normal things in the world.

The door opened and Charity was standing there, smiling widely at Faith. She was wearing a long grey dress and Faith realised it was her church outfit and she must have just got home.

"Blessed be, sister. I thought I'd never see you again," Charity choked.

"Me too," Faith said as they hugged. They were both crying. Charity glanced around. "Come inside," she said, and Faith was suddenly aware her sister was risking incurring the displeasure of the community. She hadn't been shunned, but she was not someone who they would welcome back, not now that she was non-practising. An outsider.

Charity lived next door to their oldest sister, Grace, who in turn lived two houses down from their parents. Hope lived next door to their parents on the other side. Faith just couldn't imagine it. Daniel's parents were lovely but lived an hour away and she wasn't sure either of them would want to live in each other's pockets like that.

Faith followed Charity inside and had a sudden moment of panic as the familiarity flooded back. For a moment she wanted to flee. The house was spotless of course – after all, cleanliness is next to Godliness – with only the most necessary of modern conveniences. No fancy kitchen appliances or TV. The furniture was plain and functional. There was a painting of the Last Supper over the hearth and a needlework sampler above the dining table that proclaimed 'Give thanks to the Lord, for he is good. His love endures forever – Psalm 136:1'. Faith felt a lump in her throat as she remembered Charity working on that. She had started one as well and she wondered vaguely what had happened to it. It had been something about the Lord being a rock, but she couldn't remember the exact phrase now. These were the only visible decorations aside from the large family Bible, given to every couple on their marriage, which was displayed on a table next to one of four sturdy-looking living room chairs. Nobody in the Servants of Christ had a sofa, as that would mean getting too comfortable.

"Jebediah isn't home?" Faith asked.

"He stayed behind after Worship to talk to some of the men. He'll be home soon for lunch." Charity showed Faith to a small bedroom with a single bed. There was a plain green quilt on the bed and another needlework, 'I have no greater joy to hear that my children are walking in the truth – 3 John 1:4'. Faith realised this would have been a child's room, had Charity and Jebediah been able to have them. It was the saddest thing, and almost shameful in the community, when a couple weren't blessed with children.

"Your husband – Jebediah – he's okay with me staying?"

Charity smiled at her and reached out and took her hand in her own, squeezing lightly.

"He is. He's a nice man, Faith, and, believe it or not, I'm very fond of him. Did you know he went to the technical college in Invercargill? So I guess you're not the only one who went away and got yourself all educated."

Faith looked at Charity who was grinning, just how she remembered from when they were kids, and she realised she was teasing her. "He's actually quite a modern man, for one of the Servants. Father isn't at all happy with some of the changes he's making to the egg production."

"I was hoping you might come back up north with me," Faith admitted.

"Please, don't talk like that. I'm happy with my life. I have my chores and I help out with father and of course there are Grace and Hope's children. I could never leave them. And Jebediah. I feel lucky God chose him for me and I've accepted that perhaps He chose for us to be childless so I could fulfil His wishes in other ways."

"By caring for a sick old man?"

"Not just that. Grace gets tired very easily and needs help."

"She has five, doesn't she?" Faith knew there was no point suggesting her sister should have bred less, and it would be a little insensitive to say so to Charity anyway. Grace had always played the helpless female role well, Faith recalled. She did feel a bit sad she'd never got to know any of her nieces or nephews.

"Yes, four girls and a boy. The same as mother and father. Hope has two of each."

She helped Charity set out lunch. As it was Sunday and a day of rest there was no cooking or other work allowed and Charity had roasted a chicken and baked bread the day before. There was cheese, made by the community and popular locally, but not nationwide, and tomatoes from the garden. It was a nice, simple meal, as all meals were here and although she enjoyed it, Faith couldn't help think about how she'd have missed out on things like Brie and hummus if she'd never left. And Thai takeaways and pizza too, she mused.

Jebediah arrived home and Faith heard him in the living room. She didn't expect he'd come into the kitchen, as men rarely did, and she trailed after Charity with the basket of bread.

Her brother-in-law looked up from where he stood, near the table, and for a long moment they just stared at each other warily.

"Greetings, sister, may the Lord show you favour," he said finally. Faith found herself letting out a breath she hadn't realised she'd been holding. If he had greeted her by name or even, as she'd expected, with no title at all, she would have known she wasn't really welcome. Calling her 'sister' meant that he still saw her as that: his sister-in-law. It was a small relief.

"May the Lord give you mercy," she automatically replied. Unexpectedly Jebediah gave her a shy smile. "Charity has talked of nothing but your visit since you called. You are welcome here with us, I hope you know that."

"Thank you, brother." It was amazing how Faith could just fall back to the old greetings.

They sat down for lunch and Jebediah said a short prayer, way shorter than the rambling sermon her father had given before Sunday lunch each week. He told Charity a funny story about Brother Wilson, and how he had farted during the meeting and blamed the squeaky chair. Charity giggled and he grinned back. Faith watched them with interest.

Sunday after lunch was typically a time of reflection and that had meant Bible readings from their father, and one of the children would be chosen to recite the weekly psalm. Faith had always dreaded when it was her turn as she was terrible at learning them. Luckily, being the youngest had meant a certain lenience her brother and sisters hadn't had. Strangely, on reflection, Isaac had always been the best at them, reciting word for word and with the exact intonation their father expected. She was surprised when Jebediah picked up a book and Charity took out some knitting. Not a Bible reading to be seen or heard.

"Grace's third, Naomi, is due to have her first baby next month," Charity said as she deftly clicked the needles. "Hope's daughter, Magdalene, is due to be betrothed soon so I suppose I'll be doing this for a while." She sounded resigned, not sad that others were having babies and not her. Perhaps after years of seeing the women in the community bring up their hordes of children, it was even a bit of a relief not to have them forced upon her.

"You always were skilled with your crafts," Faith told her. "Unlike me, two left hands, that's what mother always said."

"I remember your bread," Charity giggled. "We really should have thrown it out, but father said that it was wasteful so we'd have to eat it. It was like chewing on cement."

"Father would tell me to pray over it next time and I'd improve. When I didn't, he'd say the Lord must have had more important things to worry about that day."

They both chuckled.

"How is he? Is he really that sick?"

Charity put her knitting down. "With the Lord's will, it won't be long. He's grumpy every day he wakes and is still here."

"As are we all when we hear that once again he hasn't left us," Jebediah added to Faith's surprise, looking up from his book.

"Jeb, may He forgive you your shortcomings." But Charity was smiling down into her lap as she picked her knitting up and the click clack continued. Jebediah carried on reading as though he hadn't spoken at all.

"I can only imagine, he's always been eager to be called home." The community believed that there was no greater honour than death, and therefore salvation. "Do you think I could see him? I was thinking I might go over this afternoon."

Charity regarded Faith carefully, the knitting needles not stopping this time. "That's why you're here, I guess, to make your peace with him, but I wouldn't expect too much, sister. I haven't heard him say your name since you left. Do it for yourself, make peace for you."

Faith nodded. She tidied the kitchen and then changed into the skirt she'd bought in Invercargill for the purpose. It fell to her ankles and she had purposefully not worn anything like it since she'd left all those years ago. It felt strange, like she was betraying her current life somehow.

"I'll come with you," Charity said as Faith came back into

the living room. She tied a scarf over her long hair and offered one to Faith who shook her head, and they walked the short distance to their childhood home.

"It's strange, coming back," Faith said, eyeing the house as they walked up the path. It was exactly as she remembered, the same white weatherboard house with dark-green trim. The apple tree on the front lawn was bigger, the grass neatly cut — thanks to Samuel, Hope's son, Charity told her. Her palms felt sweaty and she wiped them on her skirt nervously as they approached the door.

"I've told them you're coming but don't expect too much. You know they're not going to welcome you with open arms," Charity warned.

Faith followed Charity and stopped dead in the living room doorway. She was sure her mother was wearing the exact same Sunday dress she'd been wearing twenty years ago. She'd aged, of course, was plumper, greyer and more wrinkled.

"May the Lord show you favour," Charity said.

"May the Lord give you mercy," their mother replied, not looking at Faith.

"May the Lord show you favour," Faith blurted. Her mother didn't reply.

"Daughter, make your father a cup of tea," she said, addressing Charity. Wordlessly Charity went into the kitchen. Faith gazed around. Tears pricked at her eyes and she felt like crying. The house seemed to be unchanged. The same worn chairs with the scratchy brown fabric. The old oak sideboard that had belonged to Faith's great-grandfather with the huge family Bible sitting on top of it. She wondered if her and Isaac's names had been crossed out of it. There was a tapestry of a very solemn Mary with the baby Jesus and a plain wooden cross decorating the walls, just as they'd been all Faith's childhood. Even the smell of linseed oil was the same. She'd never been able to use it, instead choosing a lemon furniture polish for her own house.

"Mother," she said. She sounded as though she were pleading.

"You weren't invited here. Why did you come?"

"I had to come, I had to say goodbye. Do you think he'll see me?" At least her mother had said not invited rather than not welcome.

"I won't stop you from seeing him, by the grace of the Almighty. He's in his room."

Faith turned but was stopped by her mother's voice. "You look well, daughter."

She wanted to throw herself at her mother like she had when she was young, to feel her plump arms around her, but instead she just nodded, afraid she'd burst into tears if she tried to speak.

The hallway was dim, her footsteps echoing on the bare wood floor. Faith paused outside her parents' room and then pushed open the door. She was assaulted by the awful smell of old person and that sweet, cloying stench of sickness.

"Father," she said quietly.

The man lying in the single bed near the window wasn't her father. Her father had been a big man, tall and solid. He'd had a shock of almost black hair and a thick beard. His eyes had been sharp and vibrant. This man was small and shrivelled, with sparse grey hair, his beard white and patchy. The eyes that peered back at her distrustfully were the same though. He turned his head towards the wall.

"May the Lord show you favour," she almost whispered.

There was no reply. Her father continued to stare at the wall. Faith reluctantly moved closer and took a seat next to his bed. The chair was one from the dining room table.

She sat there for what seemed like ages. Really, it was probably no more than five minutes. Faith thought of all the things she should say to him but nothing came out. He didn't look at her and didn't utter a word. In the end she stood and went back out into the kitchen.

Charity was talking to her sister Hope. The resemblance between all of the sisters had always been strong, but Hope's hair was now steel grey like their mother's. She wore it in the customary long braid which had been twisted on top of her head into a bun, and she looked just like Faith remembered her mother looking last time she had seen her.

"Oh, Faith. May the Lord show you favour." To Faith's surprise, Hope reached forward and wrapped Faith in a quick hug. "This is my youngest daughter, Magdalene. Magdalene, greet your Aunt Faith."

"May the Lord show you favour," Magdalene replied dutifully, but she was staring at Faith curiously.

"Did you see father?" Hope asked her.

"He wouldn't talk to me. I suppose I shouldn't have expected him to."

"Well, no, it would have been a shock for him to see you again too, I guess. At least you have now, should he be blessed to be taken by our Lord soon. I shouldn't say so, sister, but I'm pleased to see you."

"I'm really pleased to see you too, Hope. Is Grace here?"

Hope shook her head and she and Charity shared a look.

"Grace doesn't want to see you," Charity told her. She doesn't want any of her children to meet you either."

"Can I meet your other children? Do you have grandchildren as well?" They were interrupted by their mother before Hope had time to answer.

"I think you should go home now, daughter. It's the Sabbath and you should attend to your husband," she said to Charity. Faith noticed she didn't say the same thing to Hope.

Charity nodded and looked at Faith. "Come on then, sister, God be with you all."

"Mother, can I go with Aunt Charity?" Magdalene asked suddenly. "She was going to help me with my needlepoint."

"Sure, if my sister doesn't mind."

"Of course not, she's always welcome." Charity smiled at Magdalene. They stopped in the entrance to put on their scarves.

Chapter twenty-three

Faith enjoyed getting to know Magdalene and was happy to have met at least one of her sisters' children. Magdalene reminded Faith of herself at the same age. She was shy to start with but was soon asking questions about Faith's life. Faith showed her photos of her cousins and saw the way the girl looked wide-eyed at Becky in her jeans and Mickey Mouse T-shirt and the one of Rachel in a short dress at Daniel's birthday dinner last year.

"Their father lets them dress like that? Like regular Outsiders?" she asked.

Faith laughed. "I know it seems very strange to you. It took me a while to adjust when I left, but my husband Daniel is a great dad and he cares very much for his children. It's just different out there to how things are here with the Servants. It's not bad, just different."

Magdalene considered her for a while. "I heard my mother telling Aunt Charity that you should never have finished school. That was what started all the trouble. I wish I could have stayed at school though."

"Magdalene, you know what the sermons say about listening in on other people's conversations," Charity said somewhat half-heartedly, but Magdalene just shrugged. "It's true though, aunt. I liked school and I wished I could have stayed."

"Do you really want to do your needlepoint or did you just come over because you were curious about your Aunt Faith?"

"You know I hate needlepoint. Grandma says I have two left hands," Magdalene said, screwing up her nose. "What?" she added, when Faith and Charity both burst out laughing.

Jebediah came in from where he'd been out in the garden and Charity sent Magdalene to make tea and biscuits. Faith wanted to say something about how unfair it was that this task always fell to the girls, but because she had two daughters she realised she'd always got them to do the same thing. If she had had a boy though, she was sure she would have made sure he could cook and that he did his fair share of cleaning too. Daniel was a great cook and had always insisted he do as much as her around the house, especially once she went back to study and work.

"So anyway, how's Josiah Burns?" she asked instead.

"He married Serenity Williams six months after you left," Charity said. "They have six kids and another on the way."

"Praise be," Faith replied, faintly.

◇

Magdalene left and Faith and Charity made ham sandwiches for dinner and more cups of tea. Jebediah went back to his reading, so Faith and Charity sat at the kitchen table and caught up on their years apart. They soon got to talking about Magdalene.

"I worry about her," Charity said, frowning down at her hands. "She has such a spirit, you know? She reminds me so much of you at that age."

"She's what, sixteen?"

"Just turned eighteen. The elders are organising a betrothal and she's deeply unhappy with the idea, by God's grace. Faith ... she's talked to me about leaving the community."

Faith didn't really know what to say. "Because of the betrothal?" she asked.

"Not just that. She's a clever, curious girl and she's observant. She knows about other girls her age moving away to study. I probably shouldn't have, but I've talked to her about you. It's likely only encouraged her, and I'm not her mother, I know it's not my place. Lord grant me forgiveness."

"What does Hope think?"

"I don't know, we've never talked about it. Hope has accepted her lot but she and Lemuel don't have the same connection I have with Jeb. I get the feeling she feels frustrated she hasn't been able to have any say in the husbands chosen for her daughters. I know that Abigail isn't happy in her union."

It gave Faith something to think about. After evening prayer, they all retired to their bedrooms and, as it was still early, she gave Cliff a call to update him, talking quietly on her 'contraband' phone. He was happy to stay in Invercargill for a while and gave Faith an update about the van.

She decided she'd have another try the next day to talk to her father, but didn't want to stay longer than that. To be honest, she was ready to get home now. She called Daniel and they chatted until her battery was almost flat.

"How do you feel about leaving when Magdalene is unhappy?" he asked her.

"Not great, to be honest, but I can't just whisk her away. It feels wrong even suggesting it. I'm not sure she even knows where she wants to go or what she wants to do. You have no idea of what your options are when you're in the community. Or that you have any."

"Well, whatever you decide, I'll have your back. Think back to how you felt at that age, maybe. Would you like to have had someone help you?"

"I did, I had Mrs Paulson, Tania's mother. Gosh, imagine what my life would have been like if I'd stayed."

◇

Charity had a morning prayer group after breakfast and Faith had been thinking about Tania's mother after she'd hung up from Daniel the night before. She decided to pay her a visit. Jackie Paulson lived in a unit on the other side of town from where the community was, so she caught a ride with Jebediah in the egg van into town and then walked the rest of the way. She'd borrowed a warm coat off Charity and she needed it. She'd forgotten that feeling of chill down south that turned your feet into blocks of ice if you didn't have a decent pair of socks.

"Faith! Oh, my darling, how wonderful to see you. Tania said you might call in and I so hoped you would. Can I get you a coffee or cup of tea?"

Faith gave Jackie a hug. They clung together for longer than was probably normal. She hadn't been overly close to her friend's mother when they were at school but she might never have had the courage to leave if it hadn't been for her. She had talked to her parents about the idea of nursing college and whatever she had said had helped.

"I never got to thank you," she said now, a bit tearily.

Over tea she told Jackie about Magdalene. "I don't know whether it's my place to do anything," she said. "My family will probably hate me more than they already do if I help her."

"The ones who have rejected you will continue to do so, I've no doubt, but your sister — Charity — it doesn't sound like she's totally against the idea."

"I don't want her to get into trouble with her husband."

"He seems like a reasonable man. He's known around town as being quite approachable. I do know how you feel though. It was the same with you. I didn't want to interfere with the Servants of Christ community but Faith, you had so much potential and I wanted to make sure you were able to grab it by the balls if you wanted to take that option."

It was in Faith's nature to help people. That was the reason she'd thought she wanted to take up nursing but ended up doing social work. Really, she was in the best position to help Magdalene if she wanted it.

◇

When she arrived back at Charity's she changed back into the long skirt. "I'm going to have one more try to speak to Dad," she told her.

"Well, I'm headed there now so I'll be with you for moral support."

As they walked past her oldest sister Grace's house, Faith kept looking over, hoping to get a glimpse of her sister or maybe see her looking out the window, her curiosity having got the better of her. There was no sign. Grace had made it clear to Charity that she didn't want to see Faith and Faith knew she had to respect that.

"May the Lord show you favour," she said when her mother opened the door, and this time she received a nod. It was progress.

Charity had brought some soup she'd made that morning and Faith followed her into their father's room, standing behind her so at first he didn't see her.

"Daughter. The Lord has not bestowed favour upon me

this morning."

"No, father, perhaps tomorrow," Charity replied. The old man had been sick for years, Faith had found out, but had only been bedridden for the past few weeks. He must have thought he'd done something seriously displeasing for his Lord God to not have taken him yet.

"By the Grace of God," he muttered.

As Charity stepped forward the old man noticed Faith. He grunted but didn't say anything as Charity patiently propped him up with an extra pillow. "I've brought you some pumpkin soup, father. Shall we pray?"

"No, go, daughter. I don't want to eat. Leave me." Charity turned to Faith and shrugged as though this were a common occurrence. They started to leave.

"Not you," he said suddenly. Faith looked over and he was staring at her directly with his steely blue eyes. She gave Charity a nod to show that she was okay and went over to sit next to him.

"May the Lord show you favour," she said. He watched her for a long while. At least this time he wasn't refusing to even look at her.

"You're not staying."

Faith was unsure whether it was a question or a statement. "No, father, I have a husband and two daughters, Rachel and Rebecca, who need me."

Her father grunted. "Those are good names." He closed his eyes. "Pray with me," he said.

"Merciful God, I pray that you will show comfort to my father and give skill to the hands of his healers. Let his heart in thy grace be found and lift his soul towards thineself, should that be thine will: through our saviour, Jesus Christ. Amen."

"Amen," her father added. He closed his eyes then and Faith sat for a bit, thinking he'd fallen asleep. She stood to go.

"Daughter?"

Faith paused, one hand already on the door.

"Is he happy?"

A jolt shot through Faith. She knew he was talking about Isaac. Isaac who wouldn't be allowed to even cross the hearth of the family home. Who he had disowned.

"Yes, he is," she said softly. There was no expression on her father's face as he closed his eyes again and Faith left the room, closing the door gently behind her.

Chapter twenty-four

There was a soft knock at the door after they'd finished eating that night and Charity came back with Magdalene behind her.

"Mother said she'd been talking to Aunt Charity and she said you were going tomorrow," she said to Faith. "I just wanted to come and say goodbye." She was wringing her hands nervously and came and perched on one of the uncomfortable lounge seats.

"Does your mother know you're here?" Charity asked her. Magdalene shook her head. "She thinks I'm at my prayer meeting with Prudence Wilson. Except, I think she knows I'm here really. She gave me this and said if I saw Aunt Faith on my way to the Wilsons I was to give it to her." She handed Faith a package, wrapped in brown paper and tied with string. When Faith undid the string the paper fell away and she saw it was a plain wooden frame with a small tapestry inside, bordered by blue forget-me-nots: 'The Lord watch between you and me, when we are out of one another's sight – Genesis 31:49'.

"Tell your mother thank you. I'll treasure this."

"She worked for hours last night on it," Magdalene said, and Faith felt incredibly touched by the gesture.

"I'll make tea," Charity said. "Come into the kitchen. Magdalene, you can bring a cup out to your Uncle Jebediah.

"And her Uncle Jebediah would be very grateful for a slice of his wife's gingerbread too," Jebediah added with a smile, pushing up his reading glasses and returning to his book. Faith had seen it sitting on the side table earlier: *Every Good Endeavour – connecting your work to God's plan for the world.*

They sat with their hands around the warm mugs of tea and Faith thought Magdalene looked miserable. She reached out and gently touched her niece's arm. "Are you okay, sweetheart?"

"No," she wailed. "My father is at a meeting with the elders tonight and mother told me they're finalising a betrothal for me with Nathaniel Peters." A tear trickled down her cheek and she wiped it away angrily with her sleeve. She looked at Charity. "I can't, aunt," she pleaded. "He's near to thirty. And he always smells bad. Lord, please forgive me but it's true." She hiccupped a miserable sob.

"Oh, niece, I'm so sorry. Maybe he'll treat you well and you'll grow to become attached to him though. I can teach you to make a strong soap which could help with the body odour problem."

"I'll never like him. He kicked Prudence's dog the other day. He's just mean, aunt." Her gaze shifted to Faith and she looked suddenly determined. "Can I come with you to Invercargill? I can stay with your brother there until I find a job."

Faith wondered what on earth sort of a job Magdalene could get. Cleaning motel units maybe?

"No," Charity said firmly. "You can't stay there. It wouldn't be right." Now she was the one wringing her hands. Isaac wouldn't be considered a suitable option and Faith knew it wasn't Charity's fault that she felt like this. It had taken her some time when she'd left the community to reconcile the way she'd been brought up with how people's opinions were changing in the modern world. Although, there was still plenty of homophobia even when people had been brought up in relatively 'normal' families.

"I can't marry him. I don't want to marry anyone. I don't even know if I want to have children. Certainly not now. Please? I'm going to leave whether you take me or not."

"Perhaps ..." Faith started. She looked at Charity who was gnawing on her bottom lip and Magdalene who was watching her hopefully. "Would you consider coming back with me? We have a spare room and Rebecca would love to meet you. I can help you decide what you might like to do, go over your options with you."

Magdalene looked for a moment like she was going to start crying again but then resolutely lifted her chin. "May

God give you grace." She laughed. "I suppose I'll have to stop saying things like that."

"You don't have to completely change everything, you can still have your faith, you know," Faith said gently. "I'd make sure you don't feel like you have to do anything you're not happy with, you can make any changes you want to as slowly as you like."

Charity looked relieved and gave Faith a small smile. Faith knew she'd said what she had as much for her sister's benefit as her niece's.

"I think I'd like to go back to school," Magdalene said firmly, "and then maybe see after that."

"That's an excellent idea."

There was a sound in the doorway and Jebediah cleared his throat. "I'm off to bed, may God keep you. By the way, I'll be leaving at seven tomorrow, sister, I hope that's not too early? Charity will make sure there are some warm blankets in the back of the egg truck to ensure you have a comfortable trip."

"God keep you," Charity and Magdalene replied.

"Does the truck not have heating?" Faith asked, puzzled when he had left the room. "I can wear the warm coat and an extra pair of socks if I need to. You don't need to worry about the blankets."

Charity was looking thoughtfully after Jebediah. "No, I don't think that's what he meant," she said slowly. "I think he may have overheard us talking. The blankets I think are for Magdalene."

"Can't she sit up the front?"

"Faith, you must realise he can't be seen to be helping you with this. It'll all have to be on you when it's found she's left. Jeb would be treated harshly if it was thought he had anything to do with her leaving."

"I don't want to get Uncle Jebediah into trouble."

"I'll make sure that they know he had nothing to do with this," Charity told her. "Faith will have to carry the burden."

Faith nodded. "I know. That's fine. It'll be worth it, Magdalene, trust me."

"You need to go, niece, it's almost curfew. You'll need to be here before your uncle is ready to leave. I believe the lock on the back of the truck is faulty and he may need to fix it before he returns."

Magdalene nodded. A look of understanding passed between her and Charity. "What should I bring? I don't have much."

"We can get everything you need later," Faith said. "But make sure you leave a note for your mother."

◇

She and Charity were quiet as they rinsed the mugs and tidied the kitchen. Faith was aware she may not see her sister for quite some time. She doubted she would be welcome back again for many years, if ever, if she took Magdalene with her.

"You okay with all this? I know that you're going to have to take some of the flak when Magdalene leaves," she said.

"Is there any way you can pin it all on me?"

Charity turned and scooped rolled oats from a wooden barrel into a bowl. "Don't worry about me. It seems trite to say it will all blow over, but it will. I'll probably get a telling off for inviting you into my home but Magdalene leaving will be on you, sister." Charity gave her a sad smile and added a shake of cinnamon and some homemade apple juice from a flagon to the Bircher muesli she was making. "I can never regret seeing you again though and I know this is the right thing for Magdalene. It was the right thing for you, I always knew that, and Magdalene is the same."

Faith started to cry and Charity wrapped her arms around her. They hugged for a long time and Faith breathed in the scent of lavender washing powder, hoping to take that with her.

"I wish things were different. I wish we could see each other again."

"If the Lord wills it. Who knows what He has in store for us? Until then, we can write and still talk on the telephone sometimes. I'd love to hear how our niece is getting along."

"Of course."

"I'll leave the muesli on the bench and there's fresh milk in the larder for the morning."

◇

There was so much left unsaid, but they hugged again and Faith closed the bedroom door behind her.

Once she'd changed into her pyjamas and brushed her teeth, she hopped into bed, ignoring a weird childish urge to get down on her knees and say a prayer first. She picked up her phone, which had been charging, and called Daniel.

"Hi, love, how's everything going?"

"It's okay," she said. "I'm heading back to Invercargill tomorrow for one last night with Isaac and then I'm going to be driving home."

"Did you see your father again?"

"I did. I'll tell you about it when I get back."

"Well, no pressure to hurry or anything, but I have to say I'm really pleased you'll be home soon. I've missed you."

"Missed you too."

"The bed is kind of cold and empty without you," he continued, "and you know, it's been a while."

"Dan, it's been not much over a week," she laughed.

"Feels like longer. It'll be closer to two weeks by the time you get back. We don't usually go that long. Maybe I should fly down and meet you in Wellington and we could drive the rest of the way together. I could probably get Friday off, if that worked?"

"I hate to put a spanner in the works of your sneaky little romantic plan but that's not going to work, I'm afraid. I'll be with Anna, and I'm bringing someone else with me."

She told him about her plans to bring Magdalene home with her and, as she expected, he was completely encouraging and supportive.

"I think it will be great. I'll tell Becky in the morning, she'll be thrilled. She'll probably grill the poor girl and want to wear her long dresses but I'll do my best to discourage her."

"Hopefully that will be a short-lived phase," Faith agreed. "Remember when she made friends with Daksha and wanted a sari for her birthday? Actually, she still does. I don't think Magdalene's clothes will be as appealing for as long, somehow."

They chatted for a bit longer and then Faith remembered she had an early start. She felt reluctant to hang up. Hearing the warm, familiar sound of Daniels' voice had made her feel a bit homesick.

"Dan?" she said as they were about to disconnect.

"Mmm?"

"I've been thinking a bit about this lately. Do you feel like you were coerced into marrying me? If I hadn't been pregnant ..."

He interrupted her. "Hey, no, where's this coming from? You're my everything, Faith. With or without the girls you would have been it for me, love. I'm sorry if I've never made you realise that before."

"You're it for me too, always have been."

"As they say, it takes two. I chose not to use protection as well so you're not to blame. I've often wondered whether you'd have put up with me otherwise. I'm happy things happened like they did."

"Me too. We weren't as responsible back then, were we?"

"I think our generation thought we were invincible."

"Thanks, sweetheart, I feel better for talking to you."

"Talk soon then, love you."

"Love you too." She put the phone on the nightstand and turned off the light with a smile on her face.

Chapter twenty-five

North Shore Times:

WELL-KNOWN BUSINESSMAN CAUGHT WITH HIS PANTS DOWN

A prominent resident who runs a successful packaging company had an embarrassing incident yesterday at a local drycleaners.

The man, who has been given temporary name suppression, was captured on security footage breaking into the store late Sunday afternoon wearing only his tighty-whities.

Store owner Anish Singh told the times that Mr 'G' was a regular customer but that he had forgotten to pick up his usual weekly lot of suits.

It is believed that the man may have been intoxicated at the time and was seen prying open the front door with a crowbar before setting off the alarm.

On Monday, Anna woke up feeling like a new woman. With a new man. Kurt had left her asleep on Sunday to do the stake-out, which had proved uneventful. He and Wayne planned to try again that night. But he'd been back as the sun came up and had slid into bed from the bottom of the duvet, waking her up in the most delicious way.

It had been a long time since anyone had done that to her and she'd been embarrassingly loud, and quick. When he popped up beside her she'd have been mortified except he had the smuggest grin on his face and it had made her laugh.

She thought about him as she walked down to the bakery, grinning like a loon.

◇

Mary had pulled a chair up to the kitchen bench and was trying to roll out pastry. Her back was obviously worse.

"Hello, love," she said with a grimace. "I'm a bit behind this morning. Slept funny and it's taking me a bit to get moving."

Anna took the rolling pin from her hand.

"Go and see if you can get some better painkillers from the doctor. Or go home and lie down. I can sort things."

Mary looked like she might cry. She pulled herself up.

"You, my love, are a blessing." She gave Anna a fond pat. "I'll ring now and see if there's any appointments available for later, but if you're okay in here, I can serve sitting down for the most part."

Anna frowned.

"All right, but no getting up and down. I can make coffees as we go."

They worked easily together, working out a system. Anna found herself humming to the radio and feeling more herself than she had in years. When they had a lull, she approached Mary about the idea of eventually selling the cafe to her.

"I don't know how much you want for the place, or exactly what I'll get from the divorce, or even when, but I'm really interested. Will you think about it?"

Mary looked teary again, but she gave Anna a firm nod.

"I will. I want to jump in and say yes, right now, because I think it's ideal, but yes, we'll both think on it and make sure it's right, shall we?"

◇

At about eleven Gina came in for a coffee and Anna sat down for a break with her in one of the booths.

"So, Wayne informs me that he and Kurt are back on surveillance tonight, and I thought you might want to come over? We can have a few drinks, do a cheese board. Listen in on them on the police radio." She laughed and Anna wasn't sure if the last bit was a joke or not.

"That sounds perfect," she told her. "What can I bring?"

"Just yourself, and maybe some of Mary's sourdough," Gina said. "Come over any time after about five."

◇

Things were going so well, Anna thought as she walked home. Well, back to Kurt's, she reminded herself. She would have to work out where she was going to live if she was moving here. She'd have a look at the paper in the morning and ask around a bit.

The lawyer had rung her that morning and arranged an appointment for her in a few weeks' time. She had assured Anna that things seemed simple enough to divide up, and would get paperwork started to file. Greg would be served as soon as possible and hopefully wouldn't contest them. Anna needed to give her a retainer, however, so she rang her mum to see if they could lend her some money, feeling like a child again, and explained the situation.

Her mother seemed less shocked than she was expecting about the divorce, but was a bit baffled by the idea of her moving to the South Island.

"So it's called Bode? I've never heard of it. How many people are there? Why on the earth have you picked there?"

Anna had the strangest urge to tell her it was because she'd fallen for a man. But that was nuts. You didn't fall in love in a week, did you? And although she was madly in lust with Kurt, and he was lovely and kind and made her laugh, it wasn't just him that made moving feel right.

"It's a lot of things, Mum, but it feels really right. I feel like I can, not start again exactly, but start fresh, be me again."

Her mother sounded a bit choked up and she took a while to reply.

"Well, you always did know your own mind. But it's a long way away. Still, your dad and I have been meaning to do a trip down south for years."

"Well, give me a chance to get sorted, and then I'd love you to come and see the place," Anna said. "I think you'll both like it."

She had a shower, and got ready to head to Gina's. As she dressed, she realised her clothes were still in Kurt's childhood room. It seemed silly to go back and forward so she packed them up and put the bag on the floor of Kurt's wardrobe, hoping he wouldn't mind.

◇

She found Gina's place easily enough from her directions. They lived only a block and a half from the garage in a small townhouse complex that was fairly new. It had a small easy-care garden in the front. Inside the entranceway was a doormat that said 'Please hide packages from husband'.

Anna knocked on the aluminium front door and waited. Gina opened the door wearing leggings and an oversize cable-knit jumper. She had her hair pulled back in a cream band, with no makeup, and she looked both older and better to Anna's mind.

"Hey, come on in," she said warmly, "don't worry about your shoes."

Anna stepped into a small foyer with a painting of a buddha on it. A long table lined the wall under it with a resin bowl containing a set of keys.

She handed over the loaf of bread and they went into the compact galley kitchen where Gina opened a bottle of rosé and added the bread to an already assembled platter before carrying it into the lounge and getting comfy on the brown leather lounge suite.

Gina had great taste and the decor was very stylish and modern. The carpet was a soft cream colour and the curtains a warm russet. There was a heat pump on and the place was warm and inviting.

"Nice house," Anna said.

"Thanks. We only moved in here a few years ago. Downsized after Molly went off to uni. We were out of town a bit before. More rural. I got sick of the drive in to work."

"Do you own the salon?" Anna asked.

"Yeah. I worked in a heap of places in Christchurch first, and I really was over working for someone else but I didn't have the money to start up in a big city on my own. Then my grandmother died and left me a bit of an inheritance, and the rent here is way cheaper, so when Wayne got the chance to transfer back here, we took a chance." She took a slice of bread off the platter and dipped it in hummus. Anna did the same. "It helped that Molly got a scholarship to uni too."

"What is she studying?" Anna asked.

"Law," Gina said proudly. "She wants to get into contract law. It's all a bit beyond me, but we're super-proud of her."

"I bet. Is she your only child?"

"Yeah. One and done for me. I wasn't even sure I wanted any, but Wayne convinced me. He always goes on about that when I bag any of his other ideas." Gina grinned. "She's my proudest achievement really."

They helped themselves to more of the platter.

"So, what's the goss with you?" Gina asked. "You and Kurt managed to tangle the sheets yet?"

Anna was blushing, and Gina could tell by the look on her face that they had.

"Oh, well done," she said, clinking her glass with Anna's. "I tried to get Wayne in the mood this morning and he told me he'd take a raincheck, but I said the offer had expired." She gave Anna a grin. "He's going to have to work for it now."

Anna told her about the lawyer and that she would need to head back to Auckland and pack up. Sort her car and things.

"If you wanted some help, I could come with you? Help pack? I can always take a day or two off if need be."

Anna felt a little overwhelmed. "That is so kind of you. Thank you," she said.

"Oh no, I love Auckland. Big city. Well, for a day or two. We could have dinner down on the waterfront."

Anna gave her the date of the lawyer's appointment and they talked about flying up.

"I just feel bad leaving Faith to drive back with the van. But it would be so much easier to fly back later. Maybe we can sell it, and all fly back?"

"Yeah, ask Mary if you can put a sign in the shop. One at

the garage would be good too."

They sipped their drinks and nibbled on cheeses.

"So, speaking of, has Mary mentioned Cliff much?" Gina asked, leaning in as though someone might overhear her. Anna gave her a confused look. "It's just that there's a rumour going round that the two of them are getting it on. In secret. I'm digging for dirt."

Anna laughed. "Well, I haven't picked up on anything, but why would they be hiding it?"

"Cliff used to be best mates with Mary's husband Stanley and they had a huge falling out a few years before he died. I can't remember what it was about. A car maybe? And Mary and Cliff sort of kept up the feud. Then one day it seemed like they were over it, and Cliff went back to the bakery and Mary stopped taking her car to 'Clutha for a service, and so now everyone is wondering..."

"Well, I shall keep my ear to the ground," Anna told her with a grin.

"Ohh, speaking of, we should put the scanner on," Gina said, jumping up and opening a cabinet before fiddling with a few knobs. The static turned to voices and they could hear Wayne laughing, and then Kurt's low cadence.

"Is that legal?" Anna asked, and Gina laughed.

"Sure. Probably. Just maybe don't mention it to Kurt though."

◇

They were talking about paperwork which wasn't very interesting, but then Wayne asked: "So, what's the story, are you boning Anna then?" and Anna and Gina stopped chatting to listen in.

"Dude, I'm not telling you that. What are we? Twelve?" Kurt said with a laugh.

"Well, you seem pretty keen," Wayne said. "And she is hot — don't tell Gina I said that."

Anna looked at Gina hoping she wasn't upset but she was just grinning. "You are," she mouthed.

"Well, yeah, but I like her for more than that," Kurt was saying. "She's gorgeous, but she's also funny, and a really good person, and she's grounded, you know. Plus, King loves her." Wayne laughed loudly. "What? " Kurt said. "He's a good judge of character."

"Sounds like you might love her too, mate," Wayne said.

"Yeah, maybe I do," Kurt said softly, just loud enough for Anna to hear, and her heart was just mush, warmth flooding her at the thought that maybe he felt the same about her as she was starting to feel about him.

There was a sudden bang and then a '*Fuck, it's him!*' and the sound of a door opening, then more shouting, and Anna's heart was pounding.

"Kurt, watch out!" Wayne shouted, and Anna and Gina looked at each other in alarm.

'Do you think they're all right?" Anna said. Her voice was shaky but Gina was already up, grabbing their jackets.

"Let's go see," she said.

They took off running down the street towards the garage and Anna found herself praying to a God she wasn't even sure she believed in. 'Please let him be okay, please.'

The garage gate was open and Wayne was coming through, pulling out his baton. Kurt was running down the road after a guy in a beanie, who he tackled. There was an audible 'oof' as Gary hit the ground. Anna and Gina stood puffing, hands on knees as they watched Wayne and Kurt handcuff Gary and lead him back to the squad car.

"Shit, I'm off," Gina hissed. "Don't tell them we were listening in." She took off at a trot down the street. Anna turned and watched Kurt, her heart thumping. He saw her, and he moved Gary behind him slightly as if to protect her.

Shit, she *was* in love with him, she realised.

"Wayne, are you good to take him back to the station?" Kurt asked. "I'll secure things here and come down after."

Wayne agreed, and Kurt pushed Gary roughly into the back seat, ignoring his grumbling complaints. Wayne got in the driver's seat and pulled out and Kurt started towards the van with Anna following. They still hadn't said a word. Then he pushed her up against the van and kissed her. It was a hard, dominating kiss. Possessive. Anna's pulse raced.

"Watching you ... that was so hot," she gasped as they pulled apart. And then the van door was open, and their shirts were off and he pushed her down onto the slim bed.

She was frantic to get his pants off, struggling with his buttons and fumbling with his utility belt. Something hard was up against the small of her back, digging into her spine, and she squirmed.

"Is that your hand?' she said, wriggling to get off her leggings. Kurt grinned.

"No, I'm just pleased to see you."

Anna laughed and kissed him again, running her hands down to his arse and pulling him in. He groaned.

"Seriously though, what is that?" It was digging into her butt now.

Kurt pulled her up to sitting, and looked behind her, a weird expression on his face. Then he pulled back the fitted sheet and looked at the mattress. There was a large lump in it. Anna sat trying to catch her breath.

Kurt pulled up the mattress and his eyes went wide.

"What?" Anna asked. "What is it?"

Kurt gave her a strange look, then huffed out a laugh. "Well, it wasn't *my* hand," he said.

Chapter twenty-six

New Zealand Herald:

SMALLTOWN COPS CATCH COOK'S HAND THIEF

The severed and preserved hand belonging to Captain Cook has been returned intact to Te Papa after it was discovered hidden in a plumbing van being repaired in Bode, just outside of Balclutha. The van had gained some notoriety after students started a social media page related to it.

Senior Sergeant Kurt Baker and Senior Constable Wayne Harris also managed to apprehend the thief, who will appear in the Wellington High Court for arraignment later this week.

Gary Harwick (27) was a janitor at the museum and faces charges of theft, wilful damage and assault.

The next day was rather surreal. Several reporters arrived

in town looking for interviews and comments, and what felt like every Bode resident had turned up at the bakery needing a coffee, pie or doughnut but were really just angling for gossip. Kurt had been busy most of the day with paperwork and processing Gary to be sent back to Wellington with a guard. The van had been photographed and fingerprinted and so had Anna, along with having to give a lengthy statement.

By the time she got back to Kurt's late that afternoon she'd just wanted to crash. Kurt got home late and she'd already made and eaten a quick chicken lasagne that he heated up and scoffed, standing up at the kitchen bench while she showered.

They fell into his bed, almost too tired to speak. Kurt reached out and pulled her close to him, firm arms around her back and his face buried against her neck, and inhaled deeply.

"Anna Sinclair, you've certainly brought excitement to Bode," he said, kissing her collarbone.

Anna grinned, flipping them over until she was straddling him. "You ain't seen nothing yet," she told him, kissing a trail down his stomach.

◇

They woke up late and to the sound of Cliff coming into the house, talking loudly. Anna sat up in the bed and nudged Kurt, who groaned and turned over.

"Kurt, your dad's home," she hissed.

Out in the lounge she heard a woman's voice and then noise from the kitchen as they opened cupboards and ran the tap.

"Hey, Dad," Kurt called out, and Anna only just managed to scoot back under the duvet before Cliff bowled in, stopping short when he saw Kurt wasn't alone. He composed himself quickly as Kurt raised his head and gave him a nod.

"Morning," Cliff said, stepping back and pulling the door closed again. "Jug's on when you're ready."

Anna gave Kurt a slap on his shoulder and he grunted again. "You idiot," she said. "Now I have to do the walk of shame out there."

It was worse than she thought though. When she emerged in Kurt's fluffy purple dressing gown, Cliff was sitting at the dining table with Faith and a young girl who looked like she'd just stepped out of *Little House on the Prairie*.

King came barrelling over to greet her, so she focused on giving him lots of love for a few minutes. He turned to putty in her hands, rolling onto his back and whining sadly every time she stopped rubbing. Kurt gave an exaggerated sigh and muttered under his breath about ruining all their hard work. She grinned at him and he winked.

Faith jumped up to give her a hug. "Anna, this is my niece Magdalene," she said.

"Just Magda I think," the girl said quietly.

"I hope you don't mind, but I'm hoping she can squeeze in with us on the way home. In the van," Faith said.

"Oh man, I have so much to tell you," Anna said with a laugh. "Let me make coffee first."

◇

She and Kurt gave them a rundown on what had happened, with Faith going 'Good grief' every few minutes and Cliff going 'Bloody Nora' almost as often. Magda looked shell-shocked.

Kurt went off to shower since he needed to check back in at the station. Mary had decided to close up shop since she had a physio appointment in Balclutha and things had been a bit mad yesterday, declaring they needed a 'mental health' day.

"Kurt tells me you've been looking after the garden," Cliff said.

"Well, maybe more like raiding it," Anna said sheepishly. "Actually, I was planning to drop some herbs off to Mary for her pizza bread later today," she added, watching closely for Cliff's response. He cleared his throat.

"Oh, well, I could probably drop them to her shortly when I head down to the garage," he said.

"Perfect," Anna said. "She said she'd be home after one."

"Righto. I might just check the bees then." He disappeared out into the garden.

Kurt came out dressed in his uniform and gave Anna a kiss on her head.

"See you later?"

She nodded and he grabbed his keys before heading towards the door. Anna looked up to find Faith gaping at her.

"What is going on there then?"

Anna blushed and looked at Magda. "Tell you later," she said, getting up to have a shower.

Kurt opened the front door and gave a start. "Hey, can I help you?"

"Yeah, you can help me, you can help me by telling me where the hell my wife is," a voice demanded. Greg, Anna realised with a start.

"Well, I'm not sure she wants to see you ..." Kurt was saying as Anna arrived at the door, pulling closed the dressing gown and tightening its belt nervously.

"Well, I don't think that's any of your bloody business," Greg said, puffing up like a gorilla in a bespoke suit. He was red in the face and his shirt was badly creased, his hair sticking up at the front where he'd run his hands through it. He did that when he was nervous, Anna thought as she took him in, feeling strangely calm suddenly.

"Well, I'm making it my business," Kurt was saying, "and as this is my house, and you're here uninvited, I have every right to ask you to leave."

Anna put her hand on his arm and he turned to look at her warily.

"It's okay, really. You go, I'm okay. I think Greg and I need to talk." He didn't look convinced. "Really, go."

He left, somewhat reluctantly, glancing back at her a couple of times as he walked down the path. She watched as Kurt got into his car, Greg's presumably hired BMW parked next to it, looking wildly out of place. She waved awkwardly before inviting Greg in.

She gestured to the dining table where Greg lowered himself into a chair, looking a little confused as he took in his surroundings. Faith and Magda had disappeared into Kurt's old room, she assumed.

"You have to come back," Greg started. "I need you to," and Anna felt a surge of sympathy for him. He seemed a little lost. A boat without its rudder.

"I'm not, though, Greg. Not back to us," she told him gently.

"But I've come all this way to get you," he said. "The awards dinner is next week, and we always go to that together. What will people think if you're not there?"

He'd made no mention of love, Anna realised. No mention of their marriage, of trying to make it work. It was all for appearances.

"I guess they assume correctly that we're no longer together," she said, trying not to get angry.

"But what about me?" he asked. "What will I do on my own?"

He'd never been alone, Anna realised with a start. He'd lived at home, flatted with mates, lived with a previous girlfriend and then with her.

"Maybe this will be a good thing for both of us," she said gently. "A chance to figure out who we are, what we want." He looked a little dubious, but he nodded.

"You're really not coming back?" he said quietly. "We're done?"

She nodded. He sighed. "What will we tell the kids?" he said sadly.

"I think they've guessed," she told him, not wanting to tell him that they had realised before he had. "And they'll be okay. Especially if we can try to be civil. Keep things friendly. I'd like to think we could do that after so long together?"

He gave her a sad nod. "Are you really sure?" he asked again. Then he paused, looked around. "Whose house is this anyway? And who was that guy who answered the door?"

Anna decided now was not the time to tell him she was in love with another man.

"He's a friend who's helped me out when I was in need. You cut me off financially, Greg," she added. "That was a really shitty thing to do."

He looked sheepish. "I know. I'm sorry. I'll go in and sort things. I was just mad, and I thought if you had no money you'd ring and say you'd come back."

"I'm sorry too," Anna told him. She didn't specify why, but she was thinking of Kurt, how she would have to tell Greg the truth about her feelings for him eventually.

There was an awkward silence.

"Well, I suppose I'd better go," he said eventually. They stood and Anna wondered if she should hug him or shake his hand. It was like a formal business meeting to end an alliance.

"Drive carefully," she told him.

"Do you think I could ask that sales girl Donna to go with me? To the awards?" he asked as he reached the door. Anna gritted her teeth and tried not to roll her eyes. He was still the same old Greg.

"I think you should do what you think is right," she told him. Her tone was cold. She hoped he caught her disapproval, but suspected he would be making a phone call before he got to the main road. She arranged to get in touch about moving out of the house and they said a stilted goodbye. As she watched him get into the car and pull out, she couldn't help feeling a little glad he'd showed up and that that part was now over. It hadn't been as awful as she'd expected and dreaded, and she felt relieved.

◇

She got dressed in her activewear, planning to go for a walk later and look at possible places to rent. Faith came out and gave her a questioning look.

"You okay?"

"Yeah, good, I think actually."

Magda was still in Kurt's old bedroom so she made a quick quiche while she and Faith talked about their plans.

"Magdalene is eighteen, and it was totally her decision to leave the community, but I feel a bit like I've kidnapped her," Faith whispered. "I sort of want to get going and get her home where I feel like she'll be safe. And I think maybe she feels the same."

"I know it might sound a bit crazy, but I'm going to stay," Anna told her. She gave her a rundown on her long-term plan to buy out Mary, and how she felt like Bode could be home.

"And this thing with Kurt?"

"Well, it's early days, but, God, I don't know, it feels like ... something? Like the real deal, I guess. I really, really like him. Love him, I think."

"Oh, Anna, that's amazing," Faith said, "I hope it all works out."

"Thanks, you too. Will things be okay with you having her?" Anna said, indicating the closed door.

"Yeah, we'll be fine. I've been where she is now. So she'll have me and Daniel, who was there when I went through it, and I know Becky will be cool with it. Plus, I have heaps of connections through work to get her counselling and financial support and all those things. We'll be great."

"And, you saw your dad?"

"I did. It went about as well as you can imagine, but I think I got what I was looking for. Closure. I've said my goodbyes, and I never did that before. I know now, for sure, that I made the right decision." She grinned at Anna. "And picked the right husband." Anna laughed.

"Well, I'm glad it worked out for you, and I just want to say I'm so glad I met you, got drunk and bought a van with you."

They both laughed.

"Me too."

"And we'll stay in touch, right?"

"Of course. Absolutely no doubt." They stood and hugged for a long time. "I promised Isaac when I left that I'd be back anyway."

"Right, well, I'll walk you down to the garage," Anna said.

"Thanks. I have to say I'm not looking forward to Magda's face when she sees the van though."

Anna laughed. "Oh, my God, I forgot to tell you about Mike and the loo. You'll be thrilled. And I want to hear about the party too."

◇

Cliff came in from the garden and ended up giving them a lift down to the garage before he took off, herbs in hand, to see Mary. He'd put on cologne, Anna noted, and she laughed to herself. Gina would love that titbit.

Faith had insisted on paying the repair bill for the van, claiming she would get it back when she sold it once she got home. Magda looked less nervous and more excited at the adventure coming as she took in the beds in the back.

"Maybe I'll let you have a drive," Faith said to her, and Anna laughed at the look on Magda's face.

"Daniel is going to crack up when we arrive home in this," Faith said. "He'll probably want to have a night in it too."

"Well, no getting handsy in the back," Anna said, making Faith snort.

"You're having that bed," she told Magda, pointing at Anna's one. "No wonder you kept complaining about it being uncomfortable."

Anna shuddered. "I know, I don't even want to think about that now we know why."

"How did you even find it in the end?"

"I think I must have dislodged it when … never mind, I'm sure Magda will find it way more comfortable than I did."

◇

They took off down the road, Anna waving furiously. Eventually, when they had driven out of sight, she took out her list of properties for rent and started walking, wiping her eyes.

Chapter twenty-seven

None of the houses was great, but Anna was still feeling positive as she walked back to Kurt's. She could always talk to Mary about her spare room, at least until something more permanent came up.

She'd managed to see quite a bit of Bode as she walked around, and the town was growing on her more and more. Several people had waved out to her or said hello. She wandered slowly back towards Kurt's feeling optimistic. Cutting through a side street she came across an old wooden church, complete with steeple. It looked like something from a movie, and had a rose-lined path up to its double-doored entrance. A path to the side led to a wild and natural herb garden and behind it Anna found the wrought-iron-fenced Bode cemetery.

She wandered through the paths, reading the names on the graves and plaques. There were some as far back as the

1880s. She found Stanley Duncan's grave, well tended and with fresh flowers in a slender stone vase. She gave the headstone a pat as she passed it. A little way down she found what she assumed was Kurt's mother's grave.

On impulse, she headed back out to the roses and plucked one before returning to place it on the top of her headstone. She silently thanked the woman she hadn't had the pleasure of meeting, hoping that she would have approved of her for her son.

Then she headed back to the house, feeling warm inside despite the chilling air.

◇

She'd forgotten her key so she knocked at the front door hoping someone would be home. Kurt opened the door, looking shocked to see her, his hair a dishevelled mess.

"Are you okay?" she asked, but he was pulling her into him so tightly she almost couldn't breathe.

" I thought you'd left," he said, his voice cracking.

"What? Why?"

"I saw the van as I was coming back, and when I asked Mike he said you'd gone."

"What?"

"Well, I guess he said 'They've gone' and I thought he meant you as well, and I panicked."

Anna pulled back to look at him. He was visibly upset, shaking slightly. He gave a strangled laugh.

"I just made a total dick of myself, chasing after Faith, sirens and everything trying to catch you."

"You really thought I'd just go?" Anna said. She thought of Faith, panicking a bit and wondering what she'd done wrong, and bit back a smile.

"I don't know, you weren't in the van and then I thought maybe you'd had a change of heart and gone back to your husband. I came home and your clothes were gone and I just panicked, and I didn't want you to go without telling you how I feel." He looked so vulnerable, Anna's heart was melting into her legs.

"And how *do* you feel?" she asked softly.

"Madly, hopelessly in love with you," he said, and he kissed her.

Bode Chronicle:

DUNCAN'S DOUGHNUTS GRAND RE-OPENING

Mary Duncan, long-term resident of Bode and owner of the town's favourite cafe/bakery, has sold up shop. Duncan's Doughnuts, established in 1932 by George Duncan, started out as tea rooms and was taken over by his son Stanley in the early sixties where he began making the famous doughnuts. After his death, his wife Mary continued with the shop and it has been a town icon ever since.

Newcomer Anna Sinclair will take over the shop, and has given it a little face-lift. She will be familiar to residents since she has worked for Mary for the past year, and was the instigator of the ever-popular banoffee pie on the menu.

She was also the owner of the infamous plumbing van that turned out to be housing the pickled hand of Captain Cook, stolen from Te Papa.

Our own Senior Sergeant Kurt Baker, who is now dating Anna, was instrumental in capturing the thief and returning the hand to its rightful position.

Anna is looking forward to the new ownership. Mary, meanwhile, will be off temporarily after the big reveal – to go on honeymoon with local garage owner, Cliff Baker.

end.

About the authors

Nikki and Kirsty are sisters from New Zealand who wrote a book, and then wrote this one too.

You can find out more about us at **www.nikkiperryandkirstyroby.com**

Milton Keynes UK
Ingram Content Group UK Ltd.
UKHW042032071123
432164UK00004B/239

9 780473 603199